DAMON KNIGHT

CV

TOR

A TOM DOHERTY ASSOCIATES BOOK

CV

Copyright © 1985 by Damon Knight

A shorter version of this novel appeared in *The Magazine of Fantasy & Science Fiction*, copyright © 1984, 1985 by Mercury Press, Inc.

First printing: May 1985

A TOR Book

Published by Tom Doherty Associates
8-10 West 36 Street
New York, N.Y. 10018

ISBN: 0-312-93513-7

Printed in the United States of America

For TED and VIRGINIA THOMAS

1

When Emily Woodruff first saw Sea Venture on a blue November day, her heart jumped, and she said, "It's so *big!*" Her husband Jim, who misunderstood her or perhaps understood her in a different way, said reverently, "Nothing but the best," as if he were talking about a new car or a motor home. But none of the brochures had prepared her for this: Sea Venture was incredibly, impossibly big, looming there beyond the heads of the people like some fantastic cloud castle against the sky. The white wall curved up and back; above it were other curves, and beyond them she could see pennants snapping in the sun, and a tall white cylinder, with gulls soaring over it.

Jim was sixty-five, a pink-faced man with white hair brushed smoothly back against his skull. They had been married thirty-five years, good years, on the whole. Their children were grown, and they had grandchildren. Last August Jim had sold his dealerships for a sum that took Emily's breath away, and he said, "Let's have a real vacation. Let's run over to Honolulu for a couple of weeks and then take a cruise on Sea Venture."

Now, looking at the height she had to ascend, she said, "Jim, I don't think I can go up there."

"Yes, you by God can," he said in his other voice. Then two white-uniformed young women, one more beautiful than the other, were helping them onto the moving ramp, and up they went into the sky, like children on a Ferris wheel. When they reached the top, two other young women ushered them into a carpeted lobby, perfumed, echoing with voices. They got into a line that ended at a desk where a uniformed man took their tickets and turned them over to another man, brown-skinned and white-jacketed, who smiled and said, "Please follow me, Mr. and Mrs. Woodruff." They went down a softly lit blue corridor to an elevator that bore them up smoothly, and paused, and sighed into stillness. Then down another blue corridor that led them to a paneled door; the brown man opened it, bowed them in, and handed Jim the keys. "Welcome to Sea Venture," he said. "Your luggage will be up shortly. I hope you will have a very pleasant voyage."

Emily turned slowly. The room was smaller somehow than the pictures had led her to expect. The walls were papered in a blue-and-cream floral pattern; the carpet was royal blue. There were twin beds with quilted covers, and a window through which she could see the boarding area and the brown-hazed skyline of Waikiki beyond it. At the far end of the room there was a desk with a computer terminal and a wall screen.

Jim Woodruff was moving nervously around the room, hands in his pockets. "Why don't you take a little nap?" he said. "I'm going to go down and see what's what."

He paused at the door. "Is that all right?"

"Of course, Jim," she said.

When he was gone, Emily stood without moving for a moment, then roused herself to look into the closet. There was a little refrigerator, and there were plenty of hangers, including some nice padded ones. She hung up her jacket, then inspected the bathroom: tub, shower, toilet, and a curious thing that she supposed must be a bidet—she had never seen one. Towels neatly folded.

She went back into the room and sat experimentally on one of the beds. On the wall beside her was a panel with push buttons marked STEWARD, MAID, TV, MUSIC, AIR CONDITIONING, WINDOW. Did the window open? She pushed the button, and the window went black, as if a weightless curtain had descended over it instantly and silently. She was frightened, and pushed the button again; the blue sky reappeared. Then she realized how foolish she had been. The "window" was only a cleverly recessed 3-D television screen. She remembered the great, curving, unbroken white wall they had seen from the boarding ramp: there were no windows in Sea Venture.

Emily looked at the blue carpet between her feet. It was really very nice, she told herself, this little room in which she was to spend the next three months of her life.

2

At his desk in the Control Center of Sea Venture, the Chief of Operations, Stanley Bliss, was watching the embarkation in a bank of television screens. Bliss was a Cunard veteran, fifty-three years old, a portly man with pale blue eyes. He had been lured away by Sea Venture, somewhat against his better judgment, by a large advance in salary and a stupendous retirement plan. Part of the understanding was that he would become an American citizen; he didn't mind that, and he didn't mind the more or less permanent separation from his wife in Liverpool. What he did mind was the sheer infuriating complexity of the job he had taken on. On Sea Venture he wasn't called "Captain," and he wasn't a captain; he was the chief executive of an operation involving anywhere from nine hundred to fifteen hundred employees at any given moment. In theory and in fact he was responsible for the safety of the vessel (which was safe as houses), but also

11

he was indirectly in charge of the chefs, the bakers, the electronics crew, the maintenance department, the stewards, the publicity office and the newspaper, the entertainment staff; and as if that were not enough, he was ex officio a member of the Executive Council which more or less ran Sea Venture, or tried to run it, with its all-day monthly meetings and the endless committees in between, and the Stockholders' Meetings, and the Work Sessions, and the Planning Sessions, and, my God, the Initiatives and Referendums. . . .

The passengers he was seeing today were the usual lot, some of them San Francisco people reboarding after the layover in Honolulu, others boarding here for the first time, burnt red or brown, with flowered shirts and leis—a little more geriatric perhaps than the old *Queen*; the largest number were couples in their fifties and sixties, with a scattering up to eighty—blue-haired women tottering on canes, heaven knew why they wanted to go on a cruise, they never left their cabins except for meals, and two or three never came out at all; then there was a sizable group in their forties, taking up most of the seats in the bars; then the "younger crowd," twenties and thirties, who flocked together and were visible out of all proportion on the dance floor, the tennis courts and so on; then a forlorn sprinkling of teenagers glumly following their parents about. It was impossible to know how they had been attracted to Sea Venture in the first place; once you had got them, you had to keep them busy, entertained; give them the illusion, at least, that they were having a marvelous time.

In another bank of screens he could see the permanent residents boarding at the stern, nine hundred feet away. Their ramp went up to the loading area on the Sports Deck; it was an insult to the integrity of the hull to have the passenger entrance so low, but that was not the only compromise the designers had made.

He turned to the guest beside him. "Well, what do you think of us so far?"

Captain Hartman smiled noncommittally around his pipe. He was another ex-Cunard man, retired now, traveling on a courtesy pass. "Impressive," he said.

"The size, you mean. She is the largest passenger vessel ever built, let alone the biggest submersible vessel—or ever likely to be built, if you ask me."

"You don't think they'll go on with the programme? You're meant to be a prototype, aren't you? Isn't that what the P in POSH is for?"

Bliss grimaced slightly. "Prototype Open Sea Habitat, yes, somebody must have thought that was funny once, but not anymore. We call her Sea Venture, or CV for short. What she is is a bloody raft."

"Boarding completed, Chief," said the First Deputy, a handsome young Midwesterner named Ferguson.

"All right. Signal the tugs."

"How many tugs?" Hartman inquired.

"Six. They'll take us out about seventy miles, until we can catch the southbound current; then we're on our own. Tugs brought her all the way across the Pacific two years ago from the Kure Yards where she was built. The hull, that is; the fittings and interior work are all American."

"You're proud of her really, aren't you? I should be."

"Oh, well, you know," said Bliss. He was watching a screen on the console in front of him, the one that displayed a view of the reception lobby. Following his gaze, Hartman saw a passenger, an alert-looking young man with short dark hair, turn as he moved toward the desk and look directly into the camera.

His real name was Sverdrupp; he was born in Stockholm, educated in France, Germany, and England, trained in Israel and Central America. At the moment he had an American passport. For the past ten years he had been employed by a certain international organization which gave him occasional jobs to do and paid him very well. Two months ago he had been summoned to a meeting in Rome, in the course of which it appeared that he was being lent to another organization, not named then or ever, which required his services for this occasion only. His body was deceptively slender; his clothes were new and expensive. He had a boyish, open face, useful to him in his profession.

John Stevens, as he called himself now, gazed around with calm interest while the moving ramp carried him up into Sea Venture. He did not see the man he was looking for, but he did see several other celebrities: the video star Eddie Greaves, a former U.S. senator, a beer baron, the widow of a Greek shipping magnate. There were also several very pretty girls.

Stevens knew that his quarry had reserved a suite on the Signal Deck at the top of Sea Venture; he himself had booked a single cabin on the deck below, in a section which gave him privileges at the restaurant used by more exalted passengers. He rode decorously up into the reception lounge, presented his ticket, and followed a Filipino steward to his cabin. He investigated every corner of the room almost without thinking about it, sniffed the air, put his hand on the sweating side of the ice-water carafe, then sat down before the computer console at the far wall.

In the printer tray beside it was a little news sheet, the *CV Journal*. "WELCOME TO THE WONDERFUL WORLD OF SEA VENTURE!" it began, and went on, "If you would like to know some fascinating facts about Sea Venture, press the 'CV' button on your personal computer terminal." He did so, and found to his satisfaction that there was a program for deck plans.

On the wall screen a skeletal outline of the vessel appeared in 3-D. It rotated gently at his command, and he saw that the view he had had from the island, huge as it was, had given him a misleading impression. Seen from above, Sea Venture was an oval shape more than three-quarters as wide as it was long, wider than eight ordinary ships lying side by side.

He gave the computer another command, and saw a red dot with the legend YOU ARE HERE. He summoned up other dots for the Liberty Restaurant, the Signal Deck Lounge, the card room, the casino, the theater; the computer obligingly drew yellow lines from his cabin to each one. He blanked the screen, well satisfied. Then he turned on a commercial channel and sprawled in comfort against the headboard of the bed to watch "Wild Annie and Bill."

3

A powered wheelchair approached the moving ramp at the stern of Sea Venture, under the sign that read, PERMANENT RESIDENTS ONLY. In the chair was a very small gray-haired man; behind it was a large young man with an expressionless corn-fed face. As they entered the ramp, a young woman in a yellow pantsuit ran up beside them. "Professor Newland, I'm Ann Bonano of the Toronto Star."

"No interviews," barked the large young man.

"No, that's all right, Hal," Newland said in a surprisingly resonant voice. "I know Ms. Bonano—we met at the convention in Los Angeles, what was it, four years ago?"

"I didn't think you'd remember," she said, smiling. "Professor Newland, it's funny to find you here, and even funnier to find you going into the permanent resident section. Surely this doesn't mean—"

"No, no," said Newland, "just trying to make your job

17

harder. Sneaking aboard, to put it bluntly. How did you know I was here?''

"I was having lunch with a friend and forgot the time, and then I was in such a hurry that I got out at the wrong gate—and I looked up and saw you. One of the breaks.'' She took a notebook from her yellow bag. "As long as I've trapped you, why are you here? Have you changed your opinion about Sea Venture and the ocean habitat program?''

"No, not exactly, but I thought it would be educational. You know.''

She hesitated. "Professor Newland, let me put it another way. Our people in Washington tell us the space colony bill is going to be voted down again this year by a substantial margin. Does that mean you think it's time to give up? Do you see the ocean habitats as a viable alternative to L-Five?''

"I wouldn't put it that way,'' Newland said easily. "You know, this year or next year, it doesn't matter, we've got to go into space. The L-Five colonies are going to be built, there's no doubt about that; the only question is when.''

She scribbled a note. "But in the meantime,'' she said, "if Congress continues to fund the ocean habitat program, don't you think that will make them less and less inclined to give you any money for L-Five?''

"We'll have to wait and see. I think Congress usually does the right thing, sooner or later. I know you've followed my lectures, and I don't have to tell you what the reasons are. By going into space we'll be opening up brand-new territory, not just using up more of what we've already got. And not only that, we'll be gaining vast new sources of energy. That's vital. We've got to have the energy, for six billion people. And you can't get that energy from the ocean.''

"Some people are talking about thermal plants along the habitat lanes."

"Well, that's what I like to call a deep-blue-sea project."

She made another note. "Professor Newland, there have been rumors for over a year now of some kind of split between you and the rest of the L-Five leadership. Is there anything to those rumors?"

"We've had our disagreements, over the years. That's not surprising."

She paused. "You said you thought this trip on Sea Venture would be educational. What do you hope to learn?"

"Who knows? I'm always ready to learn something new. Talk to me again after Guam, and maybe I'll tell you."

"You're getting off at Guam, then, and flying back?"

"Yes."

"What are your plans then?"

"No plans. I'll do whatever needs doing."

She put her notebook away; they were almost at the top of the ramp. "Thank you very much, Professor Newland. I hope you have a pleasant voyage."

The open-decked boarding area was crowded with people greeting each other, exchanging packages, running back and forth. There seemed to be a good deal of hugging and kissing. A smiling Chinese steward came toward them through the hubbub. "Follow me, please, Professor Newland, and we'll get you into the passenger section without any trouble."

They had gone only a yard or two when a large brown man put his hand on the arm of the wheelchair. "Professor Newland, I couldn't help overhearing, on the ramp. It's an honor to have you with us. I'm Ben Higpen, the mayor. Here's my

19

phone number. Give me a call any time and I'll be glad to show you around."

"That's very kind of you, Mr. Higpen."

"My pleasure."

Only a few people stayed to watch Sea Venture slip away from her moorings, fussed at by four little tugs that churned the deep-blue, almost purple, water of the harbor. There was no band playing, and no one waving from the decks—no place to wave from. When Sea Venture was far enough away from the dock, two more tugs joined her amidships. The vessel slowly rotated, revealing her true size for the first time. Two tall white cylinders, only one of which had been visible before, towered against the sky. Slowly and steadily the vessel moved away from the island, out toward the bright horizon and the horror that awaited her.

4

Humming beerily to himself, Jim Woodruff unlocked the stateroom door and entered. His wife was sitting in one of the overstuffed chairs with her hands in her lap; to look at her, you would think she hadn't moved. "Em," he said with forced enthusiasm, "you won't believe this place. They've got movie theaters here, and a Turkish bath, and a shopping mall— What's the matter?"

"Nothing, dear, I'm fine."

"Well, you're tired. That's natural." He took a turn around the room, jingled the keys in his pocket, sat on the bed. "I met a nice guy in a bar—he's from Akron, he's in real estate there. We're going to have a great time, Em."

"I *am* tired, but I'll be all right after a while."

"Sure you will. You'll have plenty of time to rest. Did you have a nice nap?"

21

"I couldn't, but I will later. What was his name, the man from Akron?"

"Boyko, Bill Boyko. He gave me his card. A real nice guy. You know, Em, you wouldn't believe the clothes on some of the women you see here. I mean, fur coats, high heels, Arab pants, you name it. Talk about the Ritz, this is it. You want something from room service?"

"I don't think so. There's a lot of things in the refrigerator, in there."

"Yeah?" Jim rose and went to see for himself. Cold beer, soft drinks, fruit juice, sandwiches in plastic, cheese. He took a beer and came back. "Pretty soft," he said. "This is the life, Em, wait and see."

"Attention," said a voice. "Attention, all passengers. A boat drill will be held in five minutes. Please consult the card posted on your stateroom door to find your boat station, or ask any steward for assistance. When the alarm bell sounds, all passengers are requested to go to their stations."

Jim got up and looked at the card on the inside of the door. "Lifeboat Thirty-seven," he read. "Guess we'd better go."

"What does that mean, a boat drill?" Emily was sitting up with her hands clasped tightly together.

"It just means we have to go to our lifeboat, find out where it is and so on, so we'll know in case of an emergency. It's a routine thing, Em; they do it on every ship."

"But what do you mean, an emergency? The ship isn't going to sink, is it?"

"Of course the ship isn't going to sink. My God, Em, how could it sink, a thing this size? Be reasonable, will you?"

Her voice went high and thin. "But if it isn't going to

sink, why do they have lifeboats?'' She jumped when a bell began ringing in the corridor outside.

Jim clanked his beer can on the table. "I haven't got time to argue with you now. Are you coming or not?''

"No,'' she said. "No, you go, Jim. I can't.''

"All right, then, damn it.''

At the door, he took another look at the diagram on the card. Boat 37, it was on the port side of the Boat Deck near the stern; that should be easy.

The bell was still ringing. He got on the elevator with a bunch of other people who had a slightly embarrassed holiday air. They glanced at him and at each other with little smiles, as if to say, "This is really ridiculous, but isn't it fun?'' Their spirit began to infect him, and by the time they got down to the Boat Deck he was feeling a lighthearted excitement.

It was easy to find Lifeboat 37, because nearly the whole crowd was going there. The number was on a sign over one of two massive doors that opened off a kind of deep alcove. Stewards were waiting to help them over the sill. At the end of a short passageway was an open door in a white curving wall; they walked in and found themselves in a long yellow room lined on either side with blue-cushioned seats. Up in front was a pilot's chair and a console, with television screens and three round windows.

One of the stewards was standing up in front with a clipboard in his hand; he was Chinese by the look of him, but he spoke English like anybody else. "Now, ladies and gentlemen, if you will sit down and give me your attention please, I will call off your names in alphabetical order.''

They shuffled down the aisle, sorting themselves out. The seats were only about two-thirds filled.

"Abbott, Mr. and Mrs.?"

"Here."

The steward went down his list. There was no reply to many of the names he called, and he shook his head disapprovingly when he was through. "Now, ladies and gentlemen, I want to call your attention to the features of your lifeboat. In the unlikely event of an emergency requiring us to abandon Sea Venture, the alarm would sound and you would all come immediately to this station. In that event, I hope we would have better attendance than we had today." There was a little embarrassed laughter.

"When all our passengers are aboard," the steward went on, "the door would be closed and the lifeboat launched by pulling this red handle. The boat can also be launched electronically from the Control Center, provided the door is closed and sealed. As you can see, the lifeboat is completely enclosed and can be launched whether or not Sea Venture is submerged. If it is launched from a submerged position, the lifeboat will automatically rise to the surface and begin to broadcast a location signal. When it is on the surface, if conditions permit, the hatch you see overhead can be raised. Food sufficient for ten days is stored in the lockers overhead. Other supplies, including first-aid kits and life preservers, are also stored there. Are there any questions?"

"What happens after we get to the surface?" someone called.

"In the event of abandoning Sea Venture near the mainland or an inhabited island, the lifeboat will be navigated to safety. Otherwise the lifeboat will be picked up by a rescue

24

vessel. Are there any other questions?'' He waited a moment. ''Very well, ladies and gentlemen, thank you for your courtesy and patience. The drill is now over. Thank you.''

They all trooped out, laughing and talking.

5

The perm section, Newland discovered, was very much
different from the passenger area. Higpen met them at the
entrance and walked beside Newland's chair while Hal, silent
as usual, walked behind. The corridors here were wider, and
they were tiled, not carpeted; the apartments—they were not
called staterooms—had draped windows looking out on the
corridors; there were brass knockers on the doors. There was
a fountain in the big central square—it was not called a
lobby—and trees grew in tubs under the bright twenty-foot
ceiling, and there was a playground with children in it.
Higpen, obviously proud of his domain, showed them the
church and the synagogue, the theater, the school, the dairy,
the goat and pig farm. The animals were in neat enclosures;
they came running to look at Newland and sniff his fingers.
There were rabbits, too, and poultry.

There were many children, more than Newland had expected.

There were Boy Scouts and Girl Scouts and Sea Scouts; there was a 4-H Club. Everywhere they went, friendly people came up to talk to them.

Higpen took them to see the hydroponics farm, where endless rows of plants grew sturdy and green from tanks of nutrients: beans, peas, squash, tomatoes, onions, beets. There were long rooms full of dahlias, carnations, lilies of the valley. "We supply all the fresh vegetables and all the cut flowers for the restaurants in the passenger section," Higpen said proudly. "All this green stuff helps with the air recycling when we're submerged, too. We get four crops a year. No pests, no scale, no rust. Even the chemicals we use, a lot of them come straight out of the ocean."

Next he took them to see the fishery. Newland could not go into the pressurized area because of his heart problem, but he was able to watch on television screens. He saw workers standing beside a vast trough surging with green water, from which nets brought up silvery flopping masses of fish, some bigger than a man.

"Those there are tunnies," Higpen said. "Good eating. Those little ones, they're trash fish, but we grind them up for fish meal and fertilizer. This is our big cash crop; we process and freeze about three hundred tons a year, over and above what we eat ourselves. We process krill, too, a kind of plankton, and make fish paste out of it. You may have heard that the Pacific is a desert; well, don't believe it. You could make soup out of this sea water."

From the fishery they went to Higpen's neat apartment, where they met a friend of his, Yetta Bernstein, a stocky gray-haired woman. "What would you like?" she asked. "A glass of beer? Some wine?"

28

"I'd like a soft drink if you have one."

She brought him a 7-Up; Hal accepted a beer. "Ben, and Yetta," Newland asked, "how close is Sea Venture to being self-sustaining?"

Higpen shrugged. "Not very. It's the passenger money that supports us—the profit from that is about twelve million dollars a year. Part of that goes into amortizing the investment, along with the government subsidies, and the rest is paid to stockholders."

"The perms are the stockholders?"

"Some of them are. Some just lease space here, and we've even got a few renters—people trying it out to see if they like it. If we didn't have the passenger operation, no, we couldn't come near paying our own way. We take in about six hundred thousand dollars a year from the fishery, and another five hundred thousand from the farms and gardens, but that's a drop in the bucket."

"How many people are employed in the fishery, farms, and gardens?"

"About four hundred, in the winter."

"And you've got a permanent population of around two thousand? What do the rest of them do?"

Yetta Bernstein said, "They do all the things you'd expect people to do in a town of two thousand. We have a dentist, two lawyers, a bank and an insurance company. We have the people who own grocery stores and run the movie theater and so on. Ben owns a hardware store, and I run a book outlet."

"But then you're all taking in each other's washing?"

"No, not altogether," Higpen said patiently. "We have a lot of people here who are bringing in outside income. Sev-

29

eral database firms, for instance. We've got a guy who writes novels—you probably never heard of him, but he makes a living at it, and that money comes into the economy. We've got a very successful investment advisory service. They do their business by satellite datalink, just like they would if they were ashore, and their people can stop off in Manila and Taipei and Tokyo to see for themselves what's going on, and the travel doesn't cost them anything.''

"Even so.''

Higpen nodded. "Even so, we're not self-sustaining, let alone self-sufficient. Sea Venture is a prototype. To make it really work economically, we'd have to have a population of at least a million.''

"Do you think that will come?''

"Oh, I have mornings when I think it will. There are all kinds of plans and schemes. The one I like best is a flat construction that rides on the surface or just below it. It covers acres, it's a flexible assembly of linked modules so it just rides along like a raft of seaweed. Solar cells covering all that area—there's plenty of sunlight out here. It wouldn't need the passenger service, it wouldn't have to make any scheduled stops, it would just keep going around the gyre, around and around.''

"That's a lovely word, gyre. It reminds me of *Alice in Wonderland*, or that poem of Yeats'—'Turning and turning in the widening gyre. . . .' ''

Higpen nodded soberly. "This is the big one we're in, the North Pacific Gyre, but there are smaller ones you could get into if you wanted to. There's one north of the Hawaiian Islands, for instance. Or you could ride back and forth on the North Equatorial Current and the Equatorial Countercurrent.''

Newland looked at him curiously. "This is your dream, isn't it?"

"Sure. Sometimes when I wake up in the morning, before I open my eyes, I've been dreaming about it and I think I'm there."

Back in his room, Newland looked at the menu: there it was, an appetizer, *Paté de krill.* He ordered it, and it was delicious.

How could any man discover his own motives, or confront them honestly if he did find them? Was it merely the fact that he was now too ill to go into space, the certain knowledge that he would never get there alive, that had made him begin to doubt the L-5 program to which he had given thirty years of his life? Or, to go farther back, was it the coincidence of his name that had turned him unconsciously toward thoughts of space colonization in the first place? He had known many such coincidences. Was it the fact that his own life seemed to him to have taken on a gentle descending arc, now in his seventh decade, that had made him wonder if, after all, there might be something to be done here on Earth?

He knew the arguments, for and against. He had used those arguments, in lectures and debates, too long and often to put any great value on them. He knew how easy it was, and how necessary, to convince oneself first in order to persuade other people. He had been a scientist long before he became an advocate, and he still had the habit of skepticism toward unproved ideas, his own most of all.

Then there was the logic of events. The first prototype ocean habitat was here; it had cost two billion dollars to build, less than three-tenths of a percent of the most optimistic estimate for the first L-5 colony: and that would have been

31

only the beginning. Back and forth he went: yes, the benefits of a space colony would have paid back the original investment many times over by now. But there was no space colony, and Sea Venture was here.

6

After Newland's morning bath, Hal Winter carried him back to the hospital bed and began to work on his legs, contracting and straightening them. "Feeling okay?" he asked.

"Not too bad."

To distract himself from the pain, Newland thought about the fax last night from Marcia Sonnabend, the public relations director of L-5, Inc., in New York. "A good many questions here," she had written, "about the recent story in the Toronto Star, which has been picked up by wire services here and abroad. I send faxes of stories from the New York Times, Washington Post, and Los Angeles Examiner. At the board meeting Monday there were suggestions that this publicity is damaging to our position and that it should be counteracted soonest. Please give me your thoughts on this. John Howard of the Times, who has always been sympathetic, is willing to do a telephone interview at your earliest convenience; Time and Newsweek are also interested. If you would like to go ahead with this, please let me know so we can set up times."

One of the stories had been headlined, L-5 GURU WAVER-ING IN FAITH?

The steward brought in their breakfast, oatmeal and toast for Newland, scrambled eggs, sausage, hash browns and fried tomatoes for Hal. "What time is it in New York now?" Newland asked when they were finished.

"Quarter after one."

"They'll be out to lunch. Let's try in a couple of hours."

Hal carried him back to bed, and Newland sat up with a book on oceanography, not quite seeing the pages. After all, what was he going to tell her? If he gave an interview with all the old ringing declarations in it, would anybody believe them? Did he believe them himself? Newland honestly did not know. He was attracted by the simplicity of the perms, their quiet enthusiasm for Sea Venture. There was a striking difference between them and the space-colony enthusiasts: they lacked the mountain-climbing mystique, the fanaticism; they were simple small-town people whose town happened to be afloat on the Pacific.

He heard Hal talking quietly in the other room; presently he came in and handed Newland the phone. "She's on the line."

"Hello, Marcia? How are you?"

"Hello, Paul," said her clear voice. "You sound as if you're just around the corner. How's it going?"

"Oh, all right," said Newland. "I've been getting the grand tour. It's very interesting, but I may have overdone it a

34

little. Marcia, I'm afraid I'm just not up to any phone interviews right now.''

"I understand," her voice said after a moment.

"Will you tell the news people that I'll be in touch when I'm feeling stronger, say in a week or so?"

"Of course, Paul. Look, how would this be? Let me put together a statement and fax it over to you tomorrow morning. Just something to keep the wolves at bay. All right?"

"Yes, fine."

"Okay," she said. "Here's Olivia, she wants to talk to you."

Olivia Jessup was L-5's managing director, an old friend. Her voice was scratchy and thin. "Paul, I'm sorry to hear you're not feeling up to snuff. I won't keep you, but I just want you to know that Bronson and a couple of the others are making a stink."

"That's normal," said Newland.

"Yes, but it's serious, Paul. Bronson is politicking to get you voted out. What he'd really like is to expel you from the organization."

"I know," he said.

"All right. Do what you think best, but don't wait too long. Good-bye, dear."

Newland gave the phone back to Hal and put his book aside, not pretending to read anymore. There was a sour taste in his mouth; he was tired of all the maneuvering, the speeches, the true things that had somehow lost their truth over the years. When had it started to go wrong?

The tickle of uneasiness had begun before he was really aware of it, maybe as long as five years ago. In the beginning they had all been starry-eyed together, a great bunch, wonder-

35

ful people, brothers and sisters. And now the L-5 habitats were still drawings on paper turning yellow around the edges; what they had instead was the Manned Orbital Vehicles, MOVs, armed with laser weapons.

Maybe that was always the way it had to be. The military, first in Germany, then in the United States and the Soviet Union, had supported rocket research through the long difficult years. You had to take the money, because you couldn't get it anywhere else. If you wanted to make spaceships, you did what they wanted and kept your eye on the ultimate goal.

An old rhyme came into his head. *The rockets go up, the rockets come down. "Dot's not my department," says Werner von Braun.*

7

One of Bliss's time-consuming duties was to preside at frequent cocktail and dinner parties whose guests were chosen by the purser from among the rich and powerful aboard Sea Venture. These necessary entertainments would certainly have ruined his liver had he not adopted the stratagem of the famous Mr. Gibson, a teetotaler who had bribed bartenders to serve him chilled water in a martini glass, with a cocktail onion to distinguish the ersatz from the genuine. Since the Gibson was now a popular drink, however, Bliss had replaced the onion by a slice of sweet pickle, and this sometimes caused comment. When that happened, as it had just done, Bliss always confessed.

"What an unusual idea," said Mrs. Pappakouras, a handsome Greek lady in a flowered Paris caftan. "A pickle in a Gibson, do you call it, or a martini?"

"I call it a Bliss, actually; it's my own invention."

"Really! May I try a sip?"

"You may, certainly, but you'll be disappointed—it's plain water."

Her eyes narrowed with amusement. "Oh, you bad man! Then you are not really drinking at all?"

He told her the story about Gibson—"a government official in Washington, I believe. Funny that he should have been immortalized in this particular way. The Gibson as we know it is more or less neat gin."

William Firestein, the former senator from Colorado, who was standing beside Mrs. Pappakouras with a tall glass of Scotch in his hand, said gravely, "I've known several people in Washington who used the same device—not with a pickle, though, Mr. Bliss. And I've known several hundred who should have done it."

"Well, you know," said Bliss, "if I didn't, I'd be pickled myself."

This was about as far as Bliss went in the line of humor; it drew a polite laugh, as always. Maurice Malaval, the French industrialist, remarked with a smile, "It is very interesting how some people become immortalized, as you say. You know of course Monsieur Guillotin, who gave his name to the instrument by which he lost his head. And you know perhaps Monsieur Daguerre, who invented the daguerreotype. But perhaps you do not know Monsieur Poubelle?"

"No, who was he?" asked Firestein.

"He was the inventor of the dustbin—you would say in America, the garbage can."

"Really!"

"Yes, and in France, his name lives again every time we say, 'The garbage can is full.' "

CV

Across the room, the beer tycoon Howard Manning was talking to Eddie Greaves. "Eddie, you're getting off at Guam, is that right?"

"Yeah, man, they're going to fly me from there to Tokyo for a concert on the fifteenth. I took this trip so I could get away from the phone and, you know, work on some songs, but that phone rings all day and all night."

Manning smiled. "You can always take it off the hook."

"Yeah, and I could of done that in L.A., too. But it's a change of scene. What about you, how long you staying on?"

"I'm getting off at Guam, too; I have a conference scheduled in Manila—same date as your concert. I'll be sorry to miss it."

"Yeah, well, we can't all get lucky."

When she had had a few days to get over her nervousness, Emily began to feel almost at home in Sea Venture. A little newspaper, the *CV Journal,* was waiting for them in the printer tray every morning, and several times there were letters as well. As Jim said, the size of the room didn't matter, after all they only used it to sleep, and there were so many other places to go, so many things to do. They met a very congenial couple, the Prescotts, in the lounge one day and afterward spent a good deal of time with them.

After a week or so Jim found some card-playing companions, and then they did not see so much of him. Emily went to the health spa and to several lectures, which she found very interesting. She began to take lessons in origami and flower arrangement from Mrs. Oruma, who owned the Oriental Shoppe—"the gook nook," as Jim called it.

39

There was only one more really bad time before the horror began: the morning when the newspaper had an announcement on the first page about a temporary submersion. "In order to move into a more favorable current, Sea Venture will submerge to a depth of approximately three hundred feet at 1:00 A.M. tomorrow morning and will remain submerged for approximately seven hours. The submersion will be carried out during the night in order to cause the least inconvenience, but passengers who are up at that hour will be able to watch the procedure in lounge, Promenade Deck and stateroom screens."

"Jim, I don't want it to submerge," she said.

"It has to, to get into a favorable current. It says so right here. Besides, you knew all about that before you came."

"Yes, but I thought it wouldn't be until we got to those islands."

"Well, what's the difference, now or later? Pull yourself together, Emily."

But she couldn't do it. She went to bed early that night, and turned off the window: even that dreadful blackness was better than watching the ocean come up over their heads. She took two pills instead of one, but they did not make her sleep, they only turned her head fuzzy.

In the Control Center, Captain Hartman sat beside Bliss just before one o'clock, watching Deputy Womack at the console. The radioman—the Communications Coordinator they called him—was at the other end of the console, watching a bank of screens and occasionally talking quietly into a mouthpiece.

"I'm really interested to see this," said Hartman. "To me,

that's the most amazing thing about Sea Venture—submerging a thing this size. It's never been done before, I know. To tell the truth, I'm not certain why it's necessary.''

"Well, it's a good thing in storms, you know, but the real reason is for steering. All we've got is wind and currents, and that's enough if you don't mind taking ten months to go round the Pacific. But the currents change from one season to another, and they're always tricky east of the Marianas. If we want to get to Manila and not wind up somewhere in the Carolines, we've got to make some northing.''

"Can you really do that, just by adjusting your depth?''

"Oh, absolutely. It's the Coriolis force. Whatever current you're in, in this hemisphere, there's always another one underneath going off to starboard.''

"So if you ran too far to the north, you'd be out of luck?''

"That's about it. That's why they pay us our money, eh, Womack?''

The young deputy turned and smiled. "Yes, sir.''

"Here we go, then. All secure?''

"Yes, sir.''

"Take her to minus three hundred.''

Womack tapped keys on the console. "Watch the Boat Deck screens,'' said Bliss. For a minute or two nothing seemed to be happening; then Hartman saw that the floodlit waves were rising a little higher, and higher still; finally, with an accelerating motion, they broke over the lenses of the cameras on the hull. The screens blurred for a few moments, then cleared, and they were looking at a cloudy-green underwater world. A shoal of little fish darted away.

One by one the banks of television cameras were submerged: "E" Deck, "D,'' "C,'' "B,'' "A,'' then the Main Deck,

Promenade Deck, Upper Deck, Quarter Deck, Sports Deck, and finally the Signal Deck itself, and through the thick quartz deadlights Hartman could see with his own eyes that the water was surging up over them.

Risen again, her decks hosed down, Sea Venture moved week after week alone over the abyss. There were days of mild breezes, when the sea was a pale sun-wrinkled blue, and flying fish hurled themselves ahead in liquid arcs. Even when the seas rose higher, crashing against Sea Venture's hull with massive force, the vessel plowed ahead, steady as a table top. As the weather grew warmer, more and more bathers appeared in Sea Venture's four open-air pools, and the Sports Deck was crowded with tennis players, volleyball players, shuffleboard players.

On their television screens every day the passengers watched, with mingled shock and pleasure, the gray blizzards that were sweeping over the East and Midwest. Baltimore was immobilized under three feet of snow; there were thirteen feet in Minneapolis–St. Paul.

Christmas came when they were a month out of Honolulu; there was a huge tree in the Upper Deck lobby; Christmas carols chimed in the crowded corridors, and all the restaurants served a traditional dinner of roast turkey, mashed potatoes, candied yams, cranberry sauce, mince and pumpkin pie.

Bliss called home on a video circuit at nine o'clock that evening; it was ten in the morning Liverpool time, halfway around the world. His wife's image cleared; her hair was a new color, in tight curls around her ears. "Hallo, dear, Merry Christmas!"

CV

"Merry Christmas," said Bliss. "How are you getting on?"

"Oh, we're very well. How is your voyage going?"

"The usual," said Bliss. "Is everyone all right?"

"Oh, yes, we're all very well. Where are you now, dear?"

"We're just a day's voyage east of the date line—you can look that up on your globe. Very calm seas, good weather. Is Tommy there?"

"Yes, he is, dear, he wants to wish you a Merry Christmas."

Her image retired and was replaced by the callow visage of his son. "Hallo, Dad. Merry Christmas and so forth."

"Same to you, Son. Doing all right on the job, are you?"

"Oh, the job. Well, I quit that job, Dad. But I'm getting another very soon. A pal of mine has promised me it. There's an opening coming up right after the first of the year."

"Yes, I see. Did my parcels come all right?"

"Yes, they did, Dad, thank you very much. We're opening gifts tonight, I can't wait to see what they are. Did ours come, did you get them?"

"No, not yet, but I expect they'll be waiting in Guam or Manila. You know what the mails are."

"Yes, they're awful. That's too bad, I did want you to have my gift on Christmas day. Well, here's Mum."

His wife's face reappeared. "Well, dear, no good running up the bill for nothing. Have a happy Christmas."

"You, too. Good-bye, dear," said Bliss.

8

Marcia sent a fax of a statement for the press, as she had promised, and Newland approved it with a few minor changes. Bronson would not like it.

His troubles with Bronson, and perhaps with the whole L-5 movement, went back about five years, when he had first begun to suspect that Bronson's ties to the aerospace industry and the Pentagon were more far-reaching than he had supposed. It bothered him to know that there were people pushing L-5, not for the advancement of the human spirit, but for a share of the mind-boggling profits to be made from any large construction in space. And he knew that was naive, but once he began questioning other people's motives, it was inevitable that he should question his own. For the last year or so, whenever he was interviewed about L-5, there had been a small inner voice in his head saying, *Are you telling the whole truth?*

After the newspaper stories had appeared, of course, there was no point anymore in trying to conceal his presence on Sea Venture. He stayed out of public places as much as he could, anyhow; he disliked the way people carefully did not look at him in his wheelchair, and he disliked crowds. Even Hal was a distraction to him sometimes. He needed to be alone; he needed to think.

The human race had to do *something*. There were almost six billion people in the world, and five hundred million of them were starving. There was famine in India, Africa, South America. Acid rains were killing forests all over the Northern Hemisphere. A dozen armed and angry nations were poised with LOW systems to retaliate against any nuclear aggression. It was true that the ocean was an enormous unused resource, vaster than the land. Could it feed and house the billions more to come? Could it relieve the pressures long enough for humanity to solve its problems and survive?

The day after Christmas there was another celebration when they crossed the international date line and Sunday turned into Monday. Higpen called Newland on the phone. "They'll do some kind of King Neptune performance in the theater, but if you want to see the real thing, come over here about three o'clock."

"Thank you, Ben," he said.

In the town square they found what looked to be the whole perm population of Sea Venture. The square itself was packed except for one open lane marked off by ropes; people were sitting on metal bleachers, and others were looking out of windows on the upper level.

"You know you're one of the stars of the show," Higpen

said in his ear. "You don't mind, do you? If you're worried about anything, we can call it off."

"No, that's all right," Newland said with some misgivings.

Higpen left him in a roped-off area with six other people who greeted him shyly. "We're the greenhorns," one of them told him. "Our first time over the line—yours too? Well, don't worry—they say it isn't too bad."

Then a brass band struck up a lively tune. Down the open lane came a curious procession: first the band, high-school students by the look of them, in green and gold uniforms; then a goat in a cart, dressed in a gray jacket and trousers and wearing a hat; then two strikingly handsome people, a man and a woman, dressed in not very much, with pale-green makeup on their bodies and masks on their faces. With a flourish of trumpets, they mounted a platform in front of the fountain.

"Know all ye who are subjects newly come to our realm," cried the man, "that your fishy king and queen require and demand your fealty. If there be any here who refuse to submit, let them be taken and thrown into our briny deep."

Another blast of trumpets, and the procession came around again. This time Newland and the rest of his group, Hal included, were ushered to the head of the parade, two by two. When they reached the space below the platform, the green man waved his trident over Newland and Hal, crying, "I baptize you in the name of Father Ocean!" The woman beside him showered them both with green confetti, and then they were being kissed by a number of young women who hung garlands of seaweed around their necks.

After that there was a good deal of shouting and singing; somebody was putting on a skit, apparently, and there was prize-giving, but Newland could not make out much of it. Eventually the meeting began to break up, and Higpen came to rescue them.

"Now you're citizens of the sea," he said happily. "That means you belong to our family forever, whether you like it or not."

"Ben, I like it," said Newland.

9

The next day Chief of Operations Bliss showed him around the Control Center—it was not called the bridge—a comfortable, brightly lighted place lined with consoles and cabinets. There were four small, very thick quartz windows, the first he had seen in Sea Venture, two looking forward, one port, one starboard. For the rest, they relied on television screens.

Afterward Deputy Ferguson, who was going off shift, took him and Hal down to see the marine lab. Ferguson opened a door marked NO ADMITTANCE and held it for Newland's chair to pass through. Beyond was a tiled corridor with doors opening off either side. "This is our marine section," he said. "We're quite proud of it—a lot of very valuable work has been done here."

"Justifying the appropriations," said Newland with a smile. "What exactly do you do here?"

"Ocean charting, currents, bottom sampling, salinity and temperature measurements, pollutants, that kind of thing."

Through the open doors Newland glimpsed office desks, filing cabinets, banks of instruments. They crossed a room lined with tanks in which large, bright-colored fish lazily swam. At the end of the corridor was a heavy door, open; beyond it was a room with a large window in the far wall.

"This sill may be a little problem," said Ferguson.

"No, it's all right," Hal answered, and boosted the chair across.

"Is this a watertight door?" Newland asked.

"Yes. We're right down at the bottom of the hull here, and that section beyond the window is open to the sea. Here's Randy Geller, he can tell you more about it."

Geller came forward, a tall, pale young man with a reddish beard. He smiled politely when Ferguson introduced him. "I was just about to take a bottom sample," he said. "Maybe you'd like to watch?"

"Yes, very much."

Geller led him over to the window, through which Newland could see a gray-walled chamber. Overhead were tracks with traveling cranes, hoists and cables; below was green water that surged slowly from left to right, slapped against the wall, and surged again.

"The pressure is equalized, I suppose," said Newland; "that's why you have to have the window."

"That's right," Geller said with a surprised lift of his eyebrow. "People usually ask, 'Why doesn't the water come in and sink the ship?' We could pressurize this whole section, the way they do in the fishery, but that would mean decompressing every time we leave, and it would be a nuisance.

We can also watch what goes on in there through TV cameras, but their lenses keep getting wet; it's a convenience to have the window." He pointed to a bank of television screens, only one of which was turned on: it showed a vague greenish background against which yellow motes drifted. "This is the dredge camera; it ought to be just about at the bottom by now. It's a thousand meters here."

They watched in silence until something began to show up on the screen: a pebbled floor, gray-green at first, then brown, then purple-brown as it came nearer. Geller touched a control. "This is an anomaly," he said. "Manganese nodules. Most of them are farther southwest."

Newland was watching attentively. "How big are the nodules?"

"I'd say these are about ten centimeters. We'll see when we get the sample up." He touched the controls again; the view in the screen rotated downward slightly until they could see the leading edge of a complex metal object, greenish-yellow in the light. "Here we go." The metal edge bit into the bottom; a cloud of sediment rose. Geller threw a switch. "Now we just have to wait for it to come up." In the screen, the cloudy water slowly receded; they saw the dredge again, with tiny particles streaming downward at an angle.

"One thing I'm curious about," Newland said. "I notice that the water motion seems to be in a crosswise direction, but I assume that the camera we're seeing here is facing toward the bow. Now, if we're moving with the current, why is that?"

"Wind *and* current," said Geller.

"Well, but are the currents different on the bottom? That's what I meant to ask."

"There are no currents worth mentioning on the bottom here, but from the surface down to about a hundred meters, the direction of the current does change—it rotates clockwise in the Northern Hemisphere. So when we're moving with the current at the surface, we're dragging the cable against the resistance of that fan of crosswise currents, and when we reel it in, it comes back at an angle."

"I see. How long will it take to reel it in?"

"About half an hour, but I can show you what we got on the last grab, if you want."

Under a large half-cylinder of white-painted metal on the wall beside the window was a marble-topped table on which was spread what looked like a heap of clods and dirt. When Newland looked at it more closely, he saw that the clods were purplish granular lumps about the size of his fist; the rest was brown clay. Geller handed him one of the lumps, and he turned it over curiously. "How do these form, anyhow? If that isn't a silly question."

"No, it's a good question. Nobody knows how they form. There's one theory that the manganese is in solution in volcanic material under the layer of sediment, and it filters up somehow and condenses out at the sediment-water interface. The reason you find it in fields like this is that it only condenses around solid objects, usually fragments of volcanic rock. But you find other things inside them, too—sharks' teeth and the ear bones of whales."

"That's fascinating," said Newland. "Like pearls forming around grains of sand?"

A prim scientific smile twisted Geller's lips. "Well, not exactly."

Newland did not quite smile in return. "Could we see what's inside this one?" he asked.

"Sure, if you want." Geller took the nodule, picked up two others from the table, and took them to a machine that looked a little like a large stainless-steel nutcracker. He put the first nodule into the steel jaws, depressed the handle, and pulled out a little heap of fragments. "Rock," he said, showing Newland a triangular reddish chunk. He put the second nodule in, cracked it. "Rock." Then the third. "Well, well," he said. "Will you look at this?"

Newland bent closer. In Geller's palm, half-surrounded by fragments of porous manganese, was what looked like a cracked hollow sphere of glass. "What is it?"

"Looks like an australite. That's a real anomaly."

"I'm sorry, what's an australite?"

The horror began when Geller opened his mouth to reply. His eyes closed and he staggered. He came upright again, looking bewildered, with his hand to his brow.

"What's the matter?"

"I don't know. I felt like I was about to faint."

"All right now?"

"Sure. Never did that before." He bent to pick up the fragments he had dropped, and brushed the dirt away from the glass sphere. "An australite's a kind of tektite. Found near Australia, that's why they call them that. This one shouldn't be here."

"What are they, exactly?"

"Nobody knows that, either. They show evidence of melting and deformation, so they've got to be some kind of meteorite, but they're never found together with any kind of meteoritic material that could have melted to form them.

53

There are theories about that, too. I'm not that crazy about theories. What we need is data." He put the cracked glass sphere carefully down on the table. "Wait till my boss sees this."

10

The long murmuring corridors were carpeted in different colors, blue for port, red for starboard, shades of violet and purple in between, so that it was easy to tell where you were in Sea Venture. Stevens roamed the vessel, watching the crowds. Most of the passengers looked Middle American, overdressed and overjeweled, but there was an exotic sprinkling of saris and chadors. He sunned himself beside the pool on the Sports Deck and cultivated a nodding acquaintance with some of the young bathers. He visited the casino in the evening and lost a few hundred dollars at roulette. He sat in the lounge with the older passengers, looking at the sky and ocean in the television screens that cleverly counterfeited windows. Several times as he strolled down the corridors, he saw a gray head over the back of a wheelchair, but when he caught up, it was always an old woman.

From his room Stevens called the operator and was told,

not to his surprise, that no Paul Newland was listed among the passengers. In the interest of thoroughness, he asked for Harold Winter, the young man who was known to be traveling with Newland; Winter was not listed either.

Stevens was present for every meal in the Liberty Restaurant: breakfast, the ten-o'clock snack, lunch, four-o'clock tea, dinner, the midnight munch. The man he was waiting for did not appear. Evidently he and his companion were taking all their meals in their room. If this state of affairs continued, it would be seen as a blunder that he had not tried to book a suite on the Signal Deck; but there was nothing to be done about that now.

Meanwhile, both for his own comfort and for professional reasons, he needed a companion: to be alone in Sea Venture was to be conspicuous. For that very reason, there were few unattached women. Stevens narrowed his choice to three, all passably attractive young women traveling with their parents. In casual ways, as opportunity presented itself, he got on speaking terms with all three families. One of them took to him more cordially than the other two: Mr. and Mrs. Prescott and their daughter Julie. The Prescotts had spent some time in Europe, where Prescott had been the art director of an automobile company; they were able to share recollections of Paris, Lausanne, Madrid. In response to their delicate queries, he told them that he was a naturalized American citizen, an executive with a family-owned investment firm, taking a sea cruise for his health. In return, they intimated that the daughter, who was fair-haired and sad, was recovering from some ruptured romance. She had given up a job as a graphics designer, and thought she might paint, or go into social work.

Gradually he became a member of their group; they went to lectures together, dined together, strolled on the Promenade Deck. By occasional glances Stevens indicated that he was more than politely interested in Julie, but he made no overt gesture. Presently the parents began to display a kittenish insistence on throwing the two young people together. One evening, when the elder Prescotts had retired early, pleading fatigue ("It must be the sea air!" said Mrs. Prescott, with a girlish laugh), Stevens took Julie to the Quarter Deck Bar and spent an hour with her exchanging confidences. There had, in fact, been a tragic romance; the man had died. There seemed not to be any particular meaning in life, Julie said, but she knew that she had to go on. He took her back to her suite and left her with a European bow and a chaste kiss on the knuckles. Patience was everything; there was plenty of time.

He took her dancing on the following evening, and they stopped for a nightcap in the Liberty Bar. It was quite late. The only other customers were three couples, one drunk and argumentative, the rest too drunk to talk, and a large young man who sat by himself in a corner, nursing a tall drink. Stevens recognized him instantly from his photograph: it was Harold Winter.

Stevens took Julie home, kissed her goodnight, and went back to his cabin to think about methods. His instructions were to dispose of his victim in such a way that the crime could never be solved; it was to remain a mystery. Since it never would have crossed his mind to conduct himself in any other way, Stevens had accepted this without comment, but he had thought about it a good deal and had drawn a conclusion from it, which was that his new clients were not merely interested in the death of Professor Newland: they wanted the crime to remain unsolved, not out of any solicitude for Stevens, to be sure, but because they wanted the blame to fall on someone else. These were merely speculations, and had nothing to do with him as a professional, but he also noted that appropriations bills for the space-colony program were coming up in Congress, and it occurred to him that if the revered leader of the L-5 movement were to be murdered aboard Sea Venture, it could hardly fail to cause a public outcry which might sway a vote or two. Therefore he thought he knew who his new clients were; the knowledge gave him a certain private satisfaction.

At any rate, he wished to do his job in a way that would be pleasing to his clients, and he was beginning to see the possibility of a pattern: the young nurse-companion who never leaves his employer's side except when the latter is asleep. If that could be established, the first part of his problem was solved, that was to say, the isolation of the victim. The rest was merely a matter of ingenuity, of finding the most elegant solution.

11

Captain Hartman prowled the corridors of Sea Venture, sensing a whiff of wrongness. In the days before his retirement, when he was captain of the *Queen*, he had begun every day like this, taking each section in turn except the engineering section, the Chief Engineer's exclusive domain. He had carried a flashlight to shine under tables and counters, looking for dirt. He had looked for the obvious things, equipment not put away or not in good order, brass work dull, spoiled food in the refrigerators, but that was only a part of it; he had always been alert with some sixth sense for the wrongness that was not obvious, and more than once he had found it.

In a way he felt guilty about inspecting another man's vessel, but the compulsion would not let him rest. He had nothing to say against Bliss. Sea Venture was too big; Bliss had to delegate the inspections to his deputies; Hartman understood that. He walked the ship every day, nevertheless.

He listened to the roar of New Rock in the cabaret and saw the old folks in their dance hall, swaying to the strains of "Louie, Louie." He went down into the working alleys where the butchers and bakers plied their trades; he watched the maids coming and going with mounds of linen. He walked the Promenade Deck, with its tall angled television screens that almost perfectly counterfeited windows looking out on the ocean; he made the circuit of the Sports Deck, overseeing the cheerful tennis players and bathers, watching the oldsters at their shuffleboards. Through Deputy Ferguson he managed an invitation to visit the perm section, saw the fishery and the hydroponics farm, watched the children playing.

It would have been easy to say that it was only the difference of Sea Venture to any ship he had known that disturbed him. Bliss was quite right, it was not a ship. The *Queen* had been a floating hotel in name, but this was one in fact. Bar Bliss and himself, there was not a sailor aboard. There were no engines, only a generator for electricity; the cylindrical things that passed for sails were opened and shut by computer-operated mechanisms. The vessel had three independent inertial-guidance systems, and it got its position by satellite signal. A raft was what Bliss called it, and there was some justice in that. But he himself, aboard the *Queen*, had been nine-tenths manager and one-tenth sailor; it was not the passing of the old days that was on his mind. There was something else. He felt it; he smelled it; sometimes it was near.

Luis Padilla accepted the dishes from the sous-chef, placed them on his cart, lifted the covers to verify the contents— artichoke hearts, jellied consommé, caviar, crackers. Correct.

60

He stopped at the wine steward's for a half-bottle of Tio Pepe, then wheeled the silent cart out through the service doors, along the corridor to the elevator, up to the Sports Deck. He tapped on the door of Number 18.

"Come in!" That voice, like an overripe apricot. He entered.

She was there, in a frilly garment of no substance, very large, larger than ever, quaking as she moved. The Mrs. Emerton, almost two meters tall and weighing surely seventy kilos, her hair in ringlets. The Mr. Emerton was not there.

"Put it down, Luis dear. I'll sign later, all right? I'm just about to take my shower." She looked at him coquettishly as she disappeared into the bathroom.

On the dressing table, half-obscured by the evening gown draped over the chair, was an open jewel case. Pearls, gold chains hung over the edge of it like pirate treasure. At the end of one of the chains lay a pendant, an emerald the size of a thumbnail, winking green.

Padilla transferred the covered dishes to the table, arranged the silverware, whipped out his corkscrew and opened the bottle, sniffed the cork and set it down. He verified that everything was properly arranged before he left, with a last glance at the emerald.

It was not the first time she had allowed him such a glimpse. Mrs. Emerton was very careless, or else she was hoping to tempt him into an indiscretion. But he would never succumb. Once, when he was ten, his American teacher had come to class in a drunken condition and had sung to them a song his grandfather had taught him. It was a song that the American soldiers had sung during the Occupation. *Damn, damn, damn the Filipino, lazy, cowardly ladrón. Underneath*

61

Damon Knight

the starry flag, civilize him with a Krag, and return us to our own beloved home. He had thought that a crag was part of a mountain, and that the American soldiers wanted to crush the Filipinos by dropping a mountain on them. He had found out since that it was Krag, a kind of rifle.

The song accompanied his steps as he wheeled the empty cart back to the elevator. When he was much younger, maybe six or seven, his father had beaten him for stealing a toy in the drugstore. "We are not thieves, do you understand?" Whack. *"No somos ladrónes.* Do you understand?" Whack. "Do you understand?" It was the best lesson he had ever had. Mrs. Emerton could expose her jewels, or her body if she liked: they were both safe from the staff of Sea Venture. Padilla was whistling as he entered the kitchen.

Later, in the stewards' lounge, he sat with his friend Manuel Obregón and drank a little wine. Obregón and he were employed in different parts of Sea Venture, but they had joined at the same time and had kept up their acquaintance. They talked in a mixture of Pilipino, Spanish, and English, with many jokes and much laughter. Suddenly Padilla felt a little dizzy; his elbow slipped off the table, and he almost fell forward before he caught himself. To his horror, when he straightened up, he saw that his friend had slumped off his chair and was lying like a dead man, with a bloated face and eyes turned up.

12

Dr. Wallace McNulty, at the age of forty-nine, had had a singular notoriety thrust upon him. A garbled newspaper item about his being elected president of the Santa Barbara County Medical Society, shortly after the death of his wife of twenty years, had been published in *The New Yorker*, in one of those little quotes they ran at the ends of columns. Instead of just saying that he had graduated from the University of California, the item had gone on to list a whole lot of other states, as if he had graduated from all of them too. Dr. McNulty carried the clipping around in his wallet awhile and showed it to friends, feeling embarrassed but thinking he ought to be a good sport; he found, however, that one out of every three people would read the clipping and then blink at him and say, "Did you really—?" Then he would have to explain that it was a joke, a mistake. He threw the clipping away after a week or two, but whenever he introduced himself to people, there was always a moment when he was waiting for them to say, "Dr. Wallace McNulty? Aren't you the one who—?" He found that he was becoming suspicious of new acquaintances, and even of his own patients that he had had for years.

The opportunity to join Sea Venture had come along in an almost providential way. A friend of his, Ray Herring, had been hired as director of the medical services there, but at the last minute some family trouble came up and he had to stay in Santa Barbara. Ray asked Dr. McNulty if he wanted the job and Dr. McNulty discovered that he did. He applied and was accepted.

And on the whole, he had never been sorry. He had a little eight-bed hospital on the Upper Deck, the latest in diagnostic equipment, and three cheerful nurses. His work-load was less than it had been at home, but he was making more money, even without counting the free room and board.

One morning when he was in the middle of his usual series of earaches and sore throats, Janice came to him with the phone in her hand. "Doctor, it's an emergency—somebody collapsed down in the marine lab."

"Okay, give me that. Will you finish up with Mrs. Omura?" He walked into the next room, talking as he went. "McNulty. What's the problem?"

A woman's voice said, "I don't know. One minute he was okay, the next—"

"Is he breathing? Conscious?"

"Well, he's breathing kind of slowly. His eyes are half open, but he doesn't seem to hear when we talk to him. I think you'd better come down here."

"On my way. Cover him up with a blanket or something."

CV

McNulty put his head into the examination room where Janice was swabbing Mrs. Omura's ears. "I'm going to need a stretcher and a couple of guys. Will you—"

"Already done, Doctor. They're on their way."

"Well, hell," said McNulty, secretly pleased.

When he got to the marine section, he found a little group gathered around a red-bearded man who lay in front of a fish tank, with three or four lab coats thrown over him.

"Okay, who was here when it happened?" McNulty asked, kneeling beside the patient. He checked the airway, began to take a pulse: it was slow and weak.

"I was," said a dark-haired woman. "We were just standing here talking. He didn't say anything for a while, and I looked over at him, and he had a funny expression on his face, and then he was going down."

Later McNulty wrote in his notes: "Randall Geller, marine scientist, age 31. Collapsed in marine lab appr. 9:20 AM, Dec. 29. No evidence of trauma. EEG negative. Chem scan negative. Patient is stuporous, does not respond to stimuli."

On the following day he had another patient with exactly the same symptoms: Yvonne Barlow, Geller's boss in the marine lab. She was the dark-haired young woman he had talked to before, the one who had been with Geller when he collapsed.

McNulty was puzzled. He went back down to the lab, looked around and asked questions, hoping to find there had been a leakage of some noxious gas, but nobody had been using any such thing. The fact that Geller and Barlow had been stricken a day apart suggested a communicable disease, but if so, it was not like anything he had ever heard of. His two patients remained stuporous and unresponsive.

Late that afternoon he got a third one, Manuel Obregón, a steward. Obregón had been in the room when Barlow collapsed.

It began to look to McNulty as if he had an epidemic on his hands. He put in a call to the Center for Disease Control in Atlanta. Their computer had never heard of this, either.

13

From his position in the midst of the electrical network of the man's brain, he could see another person approaching. It was time to go; he felt the tug of new adventure. He slipped out and for a dizzy instant was only an energy pattern aware of other patterns in space, a perilous dark field that stretched to infinity. He moved to the nearest one, merged with it, slipped in, and again she experienced that incredible flood of sensory information, the vivid colors, the scents, the friction of clothes against her body, the tightness of undergarments and shoes, the sounds, the signals that told her the positions of her limbs. The shock was so great that her knees went weak for an instant and she almost fell. When she came upright again, she saw the man lying on the floor, eyes half-open, mouth slack. It was always that way when she left; she could hold them together while she was inside, and even make some simple improvements in the network of their

67

minds, but once she was gone, they felt the drain of the energy she had taken.

"Julie, are you all right?" A man she knew, John Stevens, was bending over her.

"Yes, I think so," she heard herself say. "I just felt— What's wrong with that man?"

"Some kind of seizure. Sit down here a moment, let me see if there's anything I can do."

When he came back, he said, "They've called the doctor. Are you sure you're all right?"

"Yes, I'm fine. Let's go in." She observed with fascination the changes that were taking place in her body in response to his presence, the contact of their skins, the faint male odor that underlay the scent of his cologne. She had felt something like this once or twice before, in other bodies, but never so strongly. Her heartbeat had speeded up; she could feel her cheeks flushing.

Now they were in the restaurant, where the tables were spread with spotless cloths the color of saffron, gleaming china, silver, crystal; a slender vase of flowers was on each table, and the saffron napkins stood in folded flowerlike shapes. A waiter in a saffron jacket handed them the saffron menus. She heard herself say, "I think I'll just have the sole. I'm not very hungry."

"Julie, if you're not feeling well, you really ought to go and lie down."

She felt the responses again, stronger than before. She was intensely aware of her own thighs, of the man's knees a few inches away from hers under the table. "I don't want to worry Mom and Dad," she heard herself say.

"Look, I'm not hungry either. Let's go up to my room,

and you can lie down for half an hour until you're feeling better.''

Now they were leaving the restaurant, walking down the violet corridor, passing the other people in their variegated clothes. All these sights and scents were pleasing to her, even though the host body was paying no attention to them; she wished they had stayed for dinner, to experience more of the sensations of human food which she had found so pleasurable in the past; but there would be time for that.

They were riding up in the hushed elevator—what ingenuity! Now they were walking down another corridor. The man was opening a door, ushering her inside with a broad warm hand on her back.

"Julie, dear," he said, drawing her into an embrace. Their bodies were pressed together, the soft tissues flattening; his hand slid higher on her back, his mouth came warm and moist on hers. Her eyes shuttered; her arms went around him, probing the hard muscles of his back. His tongue came gently into her mouth, and she felt herself slumping against him. The hollow organ between her legs was moistening, softening. The breath went out of her lungs; she turned her face away and pressed it into his shoulder.

"Julie—dear—"

Her heart was beating violently; the sensations were so strong that she could hardly bear them. Now he was unbuttoning her blouse, drawing it down over her arms. He unfastened her brassiere; his hands were on her breasts. Now he left her for a moment to pull back the covers of the bed; now he took off her skirt and panties, threw them at a chair. Now she was lying naked on the bed, her moist skin feeling the coolness. Through half-closed eyes she saw him undressing.

The organ between his thighs stood up stiff and glistening. Evidently this was going to be a reproductive activity, the first she had witnessed in humans. Her interest almost overcame her excitement.

And now he was kissing her body; now he was entering her; and now, now, she felt her hips bucking as the sensations rose to a level she would not have believed possible.

When the postcoital courtesies were over, they got dressed and went down to the Upper Deck Grille. Stevens, who had been concealing his ferocious hunger, wolfed down a tenderloin and a baked potato; Julie had the chef's salad.

Stevens took her to the door of her stateroom and left her, murmuring, "Tomorrow." Back in his room, he felt relaxed and cheerful, but not at all sleepy. During the middle passage of his duet with Julie, a really intriguing idea had occurred to him. There was no reason not to check it out before he went to bed. Stevens got a traveling bag from the closet, removed a soft leather case and put it in his breast pocket. He took the elevator down to the Boat Deck. He met no one in the corridor.

He chose a bay twenty feet from the elevators. The two facing entrances were heavy watertight doors. He bent to examine the lock of Number Fifty-three. It was an inconspicuous slot, obviously for a magnetic key. From his kit Stevens took a strip of plastic with a round handle and connected it to a flat black metal box. He slid the plastic strip gently into the lock, watching the lights that blinked in sequence. He withdrew the strip and put it into a slot in the box; the lights blinked again, went out, and a single green light appeared.

Stevens smiled. He withdrew the strip and put it into the lock. There was a faint hum, and the massive door opened.

Stevens entered, closed the door behind him, and bent to look at the door of the lifeboat itself. He tried the same key, and it opened. The lights and the blower came on inside. Stevens stepped in and looked around. Beside the door, as he remembered, was an access panel. With a screwdriver from his kit, he had it off in a couple of minutes. Inside was an array of switches labeled UMBILICAL, SIGNAL and so on. The last one was AUTO LAUNCH; beside it was a timer.

Stevens smiled again; he replaced the panel and left as he had come, locking both doors behind him. In all probability there was a circuit that would signal the opening of the doors on a console in the Control Center, but if anybody came to look at it, they would conclude that it was an electrical malfunction.

In his room, he lay on the bed and watched a Chinese film broadcast from Hong Kong. There were English subtitles, and also Chinese subtitles. The costumes were gorgeous. The plot seemed to concern a young woman who was masquerading as a man disguised as a woman. There was a bride, who at one point appeared with an orange lampshade on her head. The heroine spent a good deal of her time languishing in graceful postures, but every now and then she lost patience with a gang of warriors and laid them out in rows.

Then a documentary about microelectronics. Stevens turned off the television and went peacefully to sleep.

In the morning he called the operator and asked for the Washington Suite.

"Yes?" said a male voice.

71

"Professor Newland, please."

"I'm sorry, there's no one by that name here."

Next he tried the Lincoln Suite, with a similar result. Then the Cleveland Suite. Then the Jefferson Suite. The Adams Suite did not answer. He tried the McKinley Suite.

"Hello?"

"Professor Newland?"

"Who's calling?"

"This is Jack Boyle of the *CV Journal*. You know, the little newspaper we put out for the passengers. Is this Professor Newland?"

"No, I'm his assistant. Professor Newland doesn't give interviews."

"Oh, that's too bad. Well, thanks anyhow."

14

The Executive Council always met in a conference room on the Upper Deck, because it was about halfway between the Control Center and the perm section. Most of the others were already there when Bliss and McNulty arrived—the five Town Council members, Ben Higpen, the mayor, and representatives from the fishing and hydroponics sections. Yvonne Barlow usually attended to represent the marine scientists, but she was in the hospital, and the marine people had not sent anybody else.

Bliss found a seat for McNulty and then went up to the head of the table to talk to Yetta Bernstein, the Council president. Yetta had her glasses on and was fussing with the papers in front of her.

"Mrs. Bernstein, pardon me," said Bliss, leaning over. "I've got an item for the agenda, if you don't mind."

She fixed him with a steely glance. "Agenda items are

supposed to be provided ten days before the meeting. You know that, Mr. Bliss.''

"I do, yes, but this is an emergency matter. A medical problem. I've brought Dr. McNulty to talk about it.''

"What kind of medical problem?''

"A threatened epidemic.''

"All right. I'll put you down for number seven.''

Bliss said, "Thank you, Mrs. Bernstein.''

He went back to his seat. Items one through six concerned the hiring of a new mathematics teacher for the high school, problems with the air-conditioning system, a proposed change in the spring planting schedule, and similar matters. Bliss tuned out after a while.

"Item seven," said Mrs. Bernstein. "A threatened epidemic. Dr. McNulty.''

McNulty looked startled; he cleared his throat. "Two days ago," he said, "we started getting cases of what looks like an unknown infectious disease. I had two cases Monday, three more yesterday, and so far there are two new ones today. There are only eight beds in the hospital. We can cram another couple of beds in there, and maybe one more in the examination room, but that will be it. We're going to need more space, and until we find out more about this, I think it ought to be in an isolation area.''

"What kind of disease is it?" asked the dentist, Ira Clark.

"It's completely unfamiliar. The patients suddenly collapse, go into a stupor. We're feeding them by stomach tube.''

"Mr. Bliss?" said Mrs. Bernstein.

Bliss said, "Dr. McNulty has asked me to clear out a

74

section on the Upper Deck, near the hospital, and relocate the passengers elsewhere.''

"How big a section?"

Bliss raised an eyebrow at McNulty, who said, ''No use doing it halfway. I'd like about a hundred rooms—that would be Corridor Thirteen from Corridor F to K. We're going to need some nurses too.''

"Let's do one thing at a time," said Mrs. Bernstein. "Mr. Bliss, what's your feeling about this?"

"I don't see that we have much choice. It will show up on the balance sheets later on, of course."

Mrs. Bernstein's lips tightened. "Can you get that many passengers to move?"

"Oh, yes. They won't be happy about it, though."

"Dr. McNulty," said another council member, "if we give you this hospital annex, or whatever you want to call it, can you contain the epidemic?"

"Oh, no. I didn't mean that. The disease doesn't seem to be communicable after the patient collapses. There's a latency period. But I just think it would be a good idea to isolate the patients. We can't have them all over the place, anyhow."

"Any further comments?" Mrs. Bernstein asked.

"Call for a vote," said Higpen.

"The motion is to approve clearing out a section of staterooms on the Upper Deck, from—what was it, Dr. McNulty?"

"Corridor Thirteen from F to K."

"All right. In favor?" All the hands went up.

"Motion carried. Mr. Higpen, will you find out who we've got that has nursing experience, and coordinate with Mr. Bliss and Dr. McNulty?"

"Yes. I can think of three or four."

"Meeting adjourned."

As the others left, Mrs. Bernstein, Mayor Higpen and Ira Clark came toward them. "Let's go in here and talk," said Bernstein.

They sat at a circular table in the small room off the Council chamber. "Doctor, how serious is this?" Mrs. Bernstein asked.

"Hard to say. It's got me buffaloed; doesn't behave like any disease I ever heard of."

Ira Clark, a scholarly looking man, leaned forward. "What are the symptoms before a person collapses?"

"None that we know of. Well, there is one thing. A momentary dizziness or faintness a day or so before."

"What if we asked everybody to report to you if they felt dizzy? Could we isolate them that way and keep this thing from spreading?"

"Maybe. That's another can of worms, though. In a place this size, how many people feel dizzy? It's a common experience, especially in older folks."

"Would you be willing to try it?"

"Sure. Might need another hundred rooms, though."

"Mr. Bliss?"

"Gentlemen, and Mrs. Bernstein," said Bliss, spreading his hands, "I'm willing to do anything in reason, but can't we go a little slower? For the moment, at least, Doctor, don't you think a hundred rooms might be enough?"

"I guess so. If we run out, we can always ask for more space."

CV

McNulty's phone beeped; he said, "Excuse me," and took it out of his pocket. "McNulty."

He listened a moment. "Okay, I'm coming." He put the phone away and said, "Got another patient—that makes eight. I've got to go."

15

The new patient was Julie Prescott, twenty-eight. Her parents were all over McNulty with anxious questions. With them was a young man named Stevens; he and Ms. Prescott had been on the Promenade Deck when she was stricken.

"Did you notice any dizziness at the time?" McNulty asked.

"Why, yes, as a matter of fact. It was just for a moment. That's odd, isn't it, because the same thing happened to Julie yesterday."

"Where was that? What time?"

"In the Liberty Restaurant, about seven o'clock."

McNulty made a note. "Did a man collapse, near your table?"

"Yes. Really, Doctor, this is amazing."

McNulty felt a breath of cold air on his skin. He drew a cross and put a square around it. "Mr. Stevens, I'm going to

79

see if I can have you assigned to another stateroom temporarily. It'll be in an isolation corridor here on the Upper Deck.''

"Why, may I ask?''

"There's a chance that you're infected. I don't want to alarm you, but I think the best thing is to put you where we can keep an eye on you. You're traveling alone?''

"Yes.''

"Well, if you did come down with it, you wouldn't want to be by yourself.'' McNulty pressed a button on his desk. "Jan, will you call Bliss's office and see if you can get Mr. Stevens into an isolation room as soon as possible?''

"Yes, Doctor. What room is he in now?''

McNulty asked, and passed the information along. "In the meantime," he said, "it would be better if you wouldn't go back to your room. If you'll wait in the outer office, as soon as we're ready to move you, we'll give you a buzz.''

"This is very alarming, Doctor.''

"I know it is, but you look to me like a young man who can do whatever has to be done.''

"Thank you," said Stevens with a charming smile, and stood up. "Until later, then.''

The man did not wait. As he left the office, the watcher inside him was interested to note that his agitation was not expressed in the muscles of his face. His movements were natural and unhurried as he crossed the lobby to the elevator and stood aside to allow two elderly women to enter. As the elevator rose, he was thinking simultaneously of two things. One was that if, as seemed likely, he had been infected with Julie's disease, he had only a short time to work in. He could not take the risk of waiting until tonight to carry out his

80

attack. Elegance would have to go; this would have to be quick and dirty. In his mind was the image of a sleek gray-steel gun, small enough to be concealed in the palm of his hand; he was visualizing its location in a locked traveling case in his closet.

Under this, rigidly suppressed, was the image of a man, himself, lying on a hospital bed with a tube up his nose, and the thought that of all possible things, he detested illness most. He was recalling that he had decided years ago that he would prefer death to being a helpless vegetable; but he put this thought aside. At the surface of his mind there were other images: the door opens, a large young man appears— Harold Winter, Newland's companion. He raises the gun. . . .

With regret, the observer realized that it was time to go. For him, too, there were unacceptable risks. He slipped out into that fuzzy black space of floating snowflake patterns, and drifted toward the nearest one.

Mr. and Mrs. Eulan Neffield had just finished dressing for dinner when there was a tap at the door. "Yes?" said Mr. Neffield.

"Security."

Mr. Neffield opened the door: there stood a woman in uniform, with a steward and a stewardess behind her. "Mr. Neffield, we're sorry to disturb you and your wife, but there's a medical emergency, and we're going to have to move you to another stateroom."

"What's this?" said Mrs. Neffield, coming forward alertly. "You've got to move us? What for?"

"We're clearing out this corridor to make a hospital annex, Mrs. Neffield."

"Well, I never heard of such a thing! *I* am certainly not going to move."

"That's perfectly all right, ma'am, but in that case you realize that you will be surrounded by people with an infectious disease."

"Oh, my God!" said Mrs. Neffield. "Eulan, what are you waiting for?"

16

When the elevator stopped, she was still shaky and disoriented; her companion, Mrs. Murphy, was standing against the wall staring at the man on the floor and stuffing her fingers into her mouth.

"What happened?" she heard herself ask. Mrs. Murphy made an inarticulate noise.

The door slid open. "Come on," she said, taking the other woman's arm. "Let's get out, Georgette, hurry!"

In the corridor, as the elevator door closed, Mrs. Murphy said, "He just—he just—"

"Did you see it?"

"Yes, didn't you see it? He just fell down—"

"My back was turned. I felt all funny for a minute. Come on, dear, we'll have to report this to somebody."

"Is this the right floor?" Mrs. Murphy asked, looking around with a witless expression.

"Yes, the Signal Deck—see, right here. Come on, Georgette."

They passed a steward with a cart; he was raising his hand to knock on a door beside a discreet brass plate that read MCKINLEY SUITE The memory of something she had once known stirred in her, and she slipped out again, across the fuzzy void; and as the new avalanche of sensation struck him, he staggered and put his hand on the cart to steady himself. A woman was screaming, beside the body of another woman who lay sprawled on the floor, her skirts over her knees, eyeglasses beside her head.

Once he had quieted the screaming woman and turned her over to the two men with the stretcher who came to collect the other one, he was able to return his attention to his duties. The cart had been standing in front of the door for at least five minutes; the food would be cooling off, it was too bad.

He knocked on the door. Presently Mr. Winter opened it.

"Good afternoon, sir." He wheeled the cart in. "I'm sorry for the delay, but there was an unfortunate incident in the corridor. A lady was ill. I had to call for security."

"Is she all right now?"

"Yes, sir." He noticed with keen interest the small gray-haired man in the wheelchair. "Good afternoon, Professor Newland. Here is your lunch finally." He uncovered the tray and began laying out the dishes on the table.

"Did I hear you say someone was ill?"

"Yes, sir. Very unfortunate." He was near enough now, and he slipped out, moved across the void and was in again, raising his head and hearing Winter's voice: "Professor! Are you all right?"

"Yes," he said. "What's the matter with Kim?"

"He's unconscious. I'd better call somebody."

"First a woman in the hall, and now Kim. Do you suppose there's some kind of contagion?"

He did not listen to the reply; he was absorbed in the complex network of his new host's mind. He had expected that Newland would be interesting, and it was true: he was very interesting.

"Attention, all passengers and crew." The voice echoed down the corridors. In the lounges and restaurants, the casino, the shopping mall, heads turned to look at television screens. A round, serious face. "This is Chief of Operations Bliss. I have to inform you that a possibly contagious disease has broken out on Sea Venture. The illness is marked by a sudden collapse. The patients are being cared for in our hospital, and they are in stable condition. There is no cause for undue alarm. You should be aware, however, that the illness is sometimes preceded by a temporary dizziness or a fainting spell. All those who have experienced anything of this kind in the presence of someone who has collapsed are asked to report to Dr. Wallace McNulty at his office on the Upper Deck. Further bulletins will be issued from time to time. Thank you for your cooperation."

A blue-haired old woman, who heard this, put her bird's-foot hand to her mouth.

"What's the matter, Fran?" said her husband.

"Why, I felt faint, you remember—when that man fell down in the lobby?"

"Oh, my gosh. Maybe it doesn't mean anything. I guess we'd better go find out, though. Do you think?"

"Oh, dear. I suppose so. And here I thought I was going on this trip to get away from doctors."

McNulty persuaded Frances Quincy and her husband to move into the isolation section. On the way she fell down senseless in the corridor, and he had another patient. An hour later the same thing happened all over again—a man this time, Chandragupta Devi, seventy-one. He had been passing in the hall when Mrs. Quincy was stricken. In he went.

McNulty fed his notes into the office computer. He had the places and approximate times of onset of all the patients, and they formed a coherent chain. The computer displayed them in the three-dimensional skeleton of Sea Venture, with colored lines between them. The lines started in the marine laboratory, went back into the crew quarters, then up to the Quarter Deck, then here and there in the passenger section. In almost every case he could match up the time when one victim collapsed with the time the next one felt dizzy. There were a few where the times didn't match—three hours between Geller and Barlow, for instance—but that could be bad reporting or bad recollection.

What kind of epidemic was this, for God's sake? It wasn't spreading, it was being passed on to one victim at a time like the wand in a relay race. No wonder the experts couldn't tell him anything. There had never been anything like this in the world before.

17

Wednesday morning word came from Bliss's office that reporters from the networks wanted to interview McNulty. One of Bliss's deputies brought down a TV camera, and McNulty went through his paces for NBC, CBS, ABC, and PBS. It took nearly an hour. That afternoon he had the privilege of watching himself on the evening news. After disposing of a freak auto accident in Los Angeles, the peace conference in Nairobi, and the weather in the Midwest, the blond newsperson said, "Last Friday a mysterious epidemic swept the floating city, Sea Venture, now in mid-Pacific waters." An image of Sea Venture appeared on the rear screen, sparkling white under a smiling sky.

"Medical authorities are baffled. The only doctor on board is the resident physician, director of Sea Venture's health services, Dr. Wallace McNulty. We talked to Dr. McNulty earlier today by satlink."

The hideously enlarged image of McNulty's face appeared in the screen. It smiled insincerely. Watching, McNulty winced.

"Dr. McNulty, what can you tell us about the state of the epidemic on Sea Venture?"

"It's about the same," said the bloated McNulty in a creaky voice. "We're getting three to four cases a day."

"And the nature of the disease has not been identified, is that correct?"

"That's correct."

"What are the symptoms, Dr. McNulty?"

"Sudden collapse, stupor."

"In other words, the patient goes into a kind of coma?"

"Not a coma. They're semiconscious, but they don't respond."

"What medications have you tried, Doctor?"

"Broad-spectrum antibiotics. They don't do a thing." There was a great technical phrase for you—really impressive.

"Dr. McNulty, you're a general practitioner, is that right?"

"Yes."

"And before you came to Sea Venture, you had a family practice in Santa Barbara?"

"Yes, that's right." McNulty was sweating all over again, remembering how he had feared, against all reason, that the next question was going to be, "Are you the Dr. Wallace McNulty who—?"

"Doctor, do you think a medical specialist would be able to handle this epidemic better?"

"I don't know what kind of specialist. It isn't any known disease. I've consulted with epidemiologists and the top people in tropical diseases. We've run every test we can think of." Defensive. Would anybody trust their life to this man, or even buy a used car from him?

"And nothing is helping?"

"Not so far." Where was the reassurance, the fatherly glint of compassion in the eye? Why couldn't he be like the doctors on "Life Squad"?

"Doctor, what kind of help would you like from the American people?"

"Well, you could pray for us."

Great. A little touch of piety. If you can't get competent medical attention, McNulty thought, you can always pray. The blond newsperson, staring earnestly into the camera, was saying, "Meanwhile, a downed reconnaissance airplane in Tel Aviv Crater—" McNulty turned the set off.

On Tuesday there was a satellite call from the President, carried by the public television screens throughout Sea Venture. Bliss's voice was heard, but only the President's face appeared. The President was in the Oval Office, behind the famous desk with its Mickey Mouse figures. "Captain Bliss, I want you to know that the hearts of the American people are going out to you in this terrible emergency."

"That's very good to know, sir."

"And we realize, of course, that you're doing everything that can be done. We have complete confidence in you, Captain."

"Thank you, sir."

"And I've asked my staff to keep me informed of every development, day or night, and, Captain Bliss, we're having a special prayer meeting here tomorrow morning to ask for your safe recovery from this tribulation. And I know you're going to come through all right."

89

"Thank you, sir," said Bliss.

"Good-bye for now, and God bless you all."

The patients kept coming in, three a day, then four and five; the rooms in the isolation corridor were beginning to fill up. By the eighth day there were thirty-two victims. McNulty had left word with the night nurses to call him if there was any change, and every night he slept fitfully, expecting his phone to buzz, but it didn't.

On Friday things got worse. Thomas LeVore, sixty-eight, saw a woman collapse at breakfast, got up, walked out of the restaurant accompanied by his wife, and collapsed himself two minutes later. His wife, who was hysterical, said that he had felt a momentary faintness and had been on his way to McNulty's office to report. A similar thing happened to Mrs. Frank Ballantine, fifty-one, who had been near Mr. LeVore, and to Minoru Yamamoto, seventy-eight, and to four other people, all within the space of twenty minutes. Then there were no more cases until late that evening, when Mrs. Ora Abbott, fifty-nine, was carried in. Her husband told McNulty that she had felt faint in the corridor that morning—the same corridor where the other victims had collapsed—but had refused to go to McNulty's office.

On his way across the lobby the following morning, McNulty noticed that the crowd was unusually thin. People seemed to be trying to avoid each other. There was a funny smell in the air. The Madison Restaurant looked only about half full. There was something different about the sound too; there were no raised voices and no laughter.

McNulty greeted the security guard in the isolation corridor.

He looked into each of the patients' rooms, read the charts, talked to Janice for a minute, and then got on the phone to Bliss.

"Mr. Bliss, I want to check something with you. Is attendance off in all the restaurants, or just the Madison?"

"It's pretty much everywhere. Less on the lower decks. Room service say their phones never stop ringing. We've had to transfer staff to room service, but they're still running hours behind. If you hadn't rung me, Doctor, I was going to ring you. Could we do some sort of announcement that would reassure the passengers?"

"I was thinking the same thing. Listen, I know this sounds crazy, but I'd like you to tell people not to come in if they feel faint. They were dropping like flies yesterday, all in the same corridor."

"I don't quite understand," Bliss said.

"I don't either, but I do know people have been keeling over when they start to come here." He told Bliss about Mrs. Abbott. "*She* wouldn't come in, and she lasted longer than any of the others. It doesn't make any sense, but for Pete's sake let's try it."

"What would you suggest that I say?"

"Well, just that—hell, I don't know—tell them the medical emergency is under control, and so forth, and they don't have to report in if they feel faint anymore."

Bliss's sigh was clearly audible. "Very well, Doctor. I don't know if it will do any good, do you?"

"No."

Afterward, McNulty sat and examined the small, tight knot of panic inside him. The medical emergency was not under control. It was his responsibility, and he couldn't do a thing.

91

He had a growing number of patients who showed no sign of coming out of their stupor; for all he knew, they would never come out of it. It was hell looking at them in the morning—poor old Professor Newland, for instance, and that nice young couple, Julie Prescott and John Stevens, side by side, waxen and still.

18

Captain Hartman came down to breakfast as usual on Friday morning, and found himself alone in the sea of tablecloths except for a large young man seated two tables away. Presently a waiter came.

"Not much of a crowd today, is there?" Hartman said pleasantly.

"No, sir." The waiter, an Indian, did not smile.

"Orange juice, poached eggs, toast—cool the toast before you bring it, please." Hartman closed the menu. "Look, will you ask that young man if he'd mind my joining him? Not much sense in both of us eating alone."

"Yes, sir." The waiter bent over the young man's table. He looked up, smiled faintly and gestured.

Hartman walked over. "Sorry if this is an intrusion. Hartman is my name."

"Hal Winter." They shook hands. "Please sit down."

"I rather expected to be the only one here this morning," Hartman said, unfolding his napkin.

"Yes. Most people are hiding in their rooms."

"Mind my asking why you're not one of them, Mr. Winter?"

"There doesn't seem to be much point in it. My friend collapsed when we were in our room—first a steward, and then him. How about you?"

"Oh, just bloody-mindedness, I expect. I'm a seafaring man, retired now, but I've never thought much of hiding in one's room."

The waiter brought their orders. Hartman's toast was warm. Winter, he was interested to note, had a strip steak and a salad. Over breakfast Hartman chatted easily about his experiences on the *Queen*; Winter seemed entertained, and even smiled once or twice.

"Any news about your friend?" Hartman asked.

"No, he's the same. I'm doing volunteer work on the night shift—they won't let me nurse him, of course, but I can sneak in every once in a while. He doesn't recognize me."

"You're a nurse, then, Mr. Winter?"

"Practical nurse, and I'm trained in physical therapy." After a moment he added, "This is a rotten thing to happen. He was in a wheelchair to begin with. He never complained."

"It must be very hard for you."

"Yes. He's a great man. Paul Newland."

"Oh, yes, I read he was aboard. There's some controversy about it, I believe."

"There were people who didn't want him to come."

Hartman thought a moment. "Mr. Winter, as a professional man, what's your opinion of this disease?"

"I'm not a doctor." Winter tore a roll apart, his eyes unfocused. "There doesn't seem to be anything like it in the literature. Dr. McNulty is a G.P., but he's consulted with a lot of specialists, and they don't recognize it either."

"Not a mutation of some virus, like the Asian flu?"

"It doesn't act like *any* known disease."

Hartman chewed reflectively. "New things do seem to turn up. You remember Legionnaire's Disease, and AIDS, fifteen or twenty years ago?"

"And herpes. But this is different."

"Yes, I think it is. Mr. Winter, I remember reading once that some physicians can actually identify an illness by smell. Have you ever had that experience?"

Winter thought about it. "No."

"Please don't laugh. This isn't quite the same thing, but I have the strongest conviction that I can smell something in Sea Venture—not the individual patients, but the whole vessel. A scent of illness, perhaps."

"Or evil?"

Hartman put down his fork. "Have you felt it too?"

"Yes," Winter said.

"I don't suppose," Hartman said delicately, "you've had nightmares?"

"Yes."

Hartman said good-bye, left the restaurant and strolled down the corridors. The only people he met were stewards with carts; they all looked grim. The shopping mall was deserted; only the pharmacy was open. There was an eerie silence and a sort of darkness in Sea Venture now, as if the lights had gone dim, although when one looked at them, they seemed as bright as ever.

He was thinking about the first ships that carried the plague to Europe in the fourteenth century. What must it have been like to be the master of one of those ships, watching the people around him fall one by one?

New things did turn up. This might very well be something like the Black Death. Perhaps, he thought, it was something worse.

That night he dreamed that he was in a dark corridor of Sea Venture; all the lights were out, and in the yellowish no-light he saw that the corridor was occupied by a monstrous squid, with garage-long tentacles that writhed toward him like sucker-disked serpents; and he felt utmost despair, because he knew the monster was an evil that could not be killed. He woke with the smell of rotting seaweed in his nostrils.

Monday morning, while they were having breakfast, Jim's phone rang. He took it out of his pocket and said, "Yeah?"

"Mr. Woodruff, we have a collect call for you from Mrs. Morrison, will you accept?"

"Yeah, put her on." He covered the phone with his hand. "It's Debbie."

"Dad?" said the voice in his ear.

"Hello, sweetie."

"Are you all right? We've been so worried."

"Yeah, we're okay. How are the kids, how's Ted?"

"We're all fine, but what about you? We heard there was this terrible epidemic, and we've been trying to call you for days."

"Yeah, well, we tried to call you too, Sunday, but the

96

lines were all jammed." Emily was gesturing at him. "Your mother wants to talk to you."

Emily took the phone gingerly and held it half an inch from her ear. "Hello, Debbie?"

"Yes, Mom. I was just telling Dad, we've been so worried." Debbie was their younger daughter; she was thirty-five, married to a systems analyst in Boston. "Where are you, in your room now?"

"No, we're in a restaurant, having breakfast, dear. How are Robbie and Michael?"

"They're fine. Michael had the New Flu, he was out of school for two weeks, but he's okay now. Mom, don't you think you should eat in your room?"

"It's so small," Emily said.

"What?"

"The room is so small." She couldn't bear it for more than an hour or two at a time, except at night when she was asleep, because it seemed to get even smaller, as if the walls were thickening and growing inward, as thick as mossy stone, and the doors growing into the walls. "Is Michael all right now? Why didn't you tell us he was sick?"

"Well, we didn't want to worry you and spoil your vacation. When do they think they'll cure the epidemic?"

"I don't know, dear. Is Ted all right?" Ted Morrison was a pale, silent man who could not seem to stand Emily's company; on the few occasions when they had met, he had hardly said a word.

"Yes, he's fine. He's thinking of starting his own company."

"Isn't that nice!"

"Yes, and if you and Dad wanted to buy some shares, it

97

would really be a great investment. He's going to send you a fax about it.''

"That's nice, dear.''

"Well, I really wish you'd stay in your room more.''

"It's so small,'' Emily said.

"I'm glad you're okay, anyway. Let me say good-bye to Dad. You be careful, Mom.''

"Yes, I will. You too.'' She handed the phone to Jim. He listened, spoke a few words, and put the phone away.

"Some cockamamie scheme,'' he said. "Every time they call up, it's money. Eat your eggs, Em, they're getting cold.''

19

The messages flowed from Sea Venture's communications center through the antenna on the superstructure to the comsat overhead and back again:

". . . at fifteen and put it into Police Industries . . . tell Mother I'm perfectly all right, not to worry at all . . . and if we have to cancel, there's going to be big bucks going down the tube, so why don't you . . . Larry, I want this favor. I want it. Do you understand what I'm telling you? . . . Conditions here are absolutely outrageous . . . not even a real doctor, just some kind of G.P., and this guy Bliss is . . . dying and she needs you . . . if he thinks he can get away with this just because I'm out of touch . . . talked to Jim Farbarn on the Hill today, and he says . . . be sure to take your pills. . . ."

And the newspapers, faxed in every day, were full of excited headlines: CV RAVAGED BY DISEASE . . . PLAGUE MAY

99

FORCE CANCELATION OF CONCERT . . . DOOMED PASSENGERS RIOT
IN PANIC . . . FARBARN URGES PROBE OF CV. . . .

Eddie Greaves was saying to his agent in New York, ''If
we have to cancel Tokyo I'm going to be in deep shit,
Marty.''

''I know that, Eddie. I'm working on it, believe me.''

''You talk to Byers yet?''

''Yes, and he's going to take it to the White House as soon
as the President gets back from Monterey. I think we have a
good shot.''

''Good shot isn't good enough. I'm talking *deep* shit,
Marty.''

''I know that, Eddie.''

''All right, who else can we get? You talk to Greg?''

''He's in Vegas.''

''So talk to him in Vegas.''

''He's either on, or he's at the crap table, or he's rolling
some broad, Eddie. You know how Greg is. The minute he
heads back for Hollywood, I'll have him on the phone, I give
you my solemn promise. Meanwhile, look, aren't there some
folks with clout on CV? They're probably just as antsy to get
off as you are. Go talk to them, Eddie, tell them what we're
doing, find out what they can do. If we start putting pressure
on from six different directions—''

''Okay. Good idea. Okay.''

''And keep your ass sweet, kid.''

The waiter approached the nice young couple with his
carafe. ''More coffee?''

''Yes, please,'' the man said. The waiter poured hers first,
then the man's. As he turned away, something about the

woman's expression remained in his mind, and he slipped out across the cold fuzzy void in the slow motion of that place toward the starflake pattern that was hers, and as he slipped in again, the colors and scents crashed against her more strongly than ever, and she raised her head, seeing the waiter's body sprawled on the floor, the carafe rolling, coffee in a long steaming splatter almost to the next table. People were standing up to look. Her husband leaned toward her.

"Are you all right?" she said.

"Yes, are *you*?"

"Yes." But she knew better. In spite of the shock, she had realized instantly what had happened, and had known what she must do.

"Thank heaven," said Malcolm. "Let's get out of here."

"I want to go to the ladies' room first." She got up and walked out. Her perceptions were blurred; she felt choked inside with sorrow for herself, for Malcolm, for the relationship they had had together. She was thinking that it was probably the second or third time in their married life that she had told him an untruth; also that it was a good thing that she had been able to turn away quickly so that he could not see the expression on her face.

She took the first elevator going down and rode it to E Deck, where she had never been before. She was interested to notice that the corridors were narrower here, the walls and carpets plainer. The people she saw were wearing clothing which she recognized as ready-made, and they were a little younger than the passengers on the upper levels; the restaurants had plain white tablecloths, and there were snack bars with plastic chairs. It was all part of the monetary system, apparently; the people here had paid less for their passage, and therefore the furnishings were less expensive; the people were younger because younger people had less money. Was it because they were younger that they also appeared less cheerful?

She came to a movie theater, paid and went in without noticing what the film was, but the observer inside her was able to read part of the sign over the entrance: . . . IDE OF THE ROCKIES. LANCE MAHONEY. She had never seen a film in a theater before, although she had experienced many on the television screens in passengers' rooms, and deeply appreciated them as an art form as well as a wonderful source of information.

It was interesting that people would go to a theater to see films when they could see them as well in the privacy of their rooms: that was their contradictory gregariousness; they valued privacy so much that they were willing to pay high prices for the rooms whose smallness they complained of, and yet at every opportunity they sought the company of their own kind.

On the screen, a man in a checkered red jacket was paddling a canoe down a river. Her attention was not on it: she was looking at the people who sat in the darkness in couples and small groups far removed from each other—another illustration of the paradox, for she was aware that this was customary behavior even when there was no threat of infection. That was fascinating, and so was the almost uncontrollable emotion she was feeling as she sat down behind two men, one of whom had his arm around the other.

The woman knew that she was infected, although she mistakenly believed her illness was bacterial in nature; from the first moment, her concern had been that she should not pass on the infection to her husband. She believed she was

102

going to die without seeing him again, and this was the cause of the sorrow that made her whole body tremble, an emotion as pure and intense as any she had so far experienced; and yet—another paradox—it did not occur to her to gratify her wish by staying with him for the time she had left. She had not encountered this particular response before, and it struck her as beautiful as well as mysterious.

She was able to follow the plot of the movie, more or less, since her eyes remained fixed on the screen although unfocused and blurred by warm moisture: the man in the checkered shirt, who had now abandoned his canoe and was walking through the forest, was escaping from pursuers in red uniforms, "the Mounties," evidently law-enforcement officers; it was not clear what crime he was suspected of, or whether or not he was guilty. There was an encounter with some Indians and a beautiful blond girl; the man in the checkered shirt rode with them in their vehicle until some tension developed between him and their leader; then there was a fight, and the checkered-shirt man defeated all the Indians by striking them with his hands and feet, and rode away in the vehicle with the girl.

Then, by a transition she could not follow, the man and the girl were seated at a camp fire in the wilderness. Presently they got into a tent and appeared to perform a reproductive act. By the expression on the girl's face, which was shown highly enlarged, she was able to determine that the actress was attempting to counterfeit sexual emotion. It was surprising, she thought, that in the interest of realism as well as for the intense pleasure it gave the participants, the actor and actress had not engaged in a genuine act of copulation. Possibly, by convention, the act was performed only in private, in which case it was curious that it should be even simulated in public; or, perhaps, different circumstances were required.

After the film ended, with the man and the girl driving down a dusty road toward an incandescent sunset, the theater lights came up and the audience filed out. She went with them, thinking that she must find another place that offered concealment as well as the company of other people. She was feeling a dull disappointment that she had not collapsed in the theater. It would have been easy to grant her wish, but the situation was so novel that she was unwilling to leave her host until she saw how it would turn out.

In the corridor, she started when she heard a voice from the loudspeakers: "Paging Mrs. Malcolm Claiborne. Please come to the nearest courtesy phone. Paging Mrs. Malcolm Claiborne."

She was thinking how frantic Malcolm must be, of his relief if he found her. She went into a women's room and sat for a long time in a booth. "Honey, is anything the matter?" said a large woman with brass-colored hair as she came out.

"No, I'm okay. Thanks." She made herself smile.

She went into a coffee shop and ordered a sandwich, which she did not eat. She was thinking that it must happen soon now. It would be most interesting, the observer thought, to see what she did when night came.

20

It was very late, and the crowds in the corridors were thinning out. As she walked past the lighted windows of the shops in the mall, she heard a voice from a distant loudspeaker. ". . . since early this morning. When last seen, she was wearing a pale yellow skirt and blouse." In a television screen at the end of the lobby, she caught a glimpse of a photograph, a woman squinting into the camera. She recognized it as a photograph Malcolm carried; it seemed no more herself than any stranger's face.

She was thinking now with leaden disappointment that the thing was not going to leave her. She must find someplace to hide, to sleep.

What did people do who had nowhere to go? There were the lounges, but a sleeping person would be conspicuous there; probably a steward would come to wake her up. Thinking of night and air, she got into the next elevator she came to and rode up to the Sports Deck. No one was in the lobby. She opened the weather door and stepped out onto the deserted tennis area. The moon and stars were brilliant in a Prussian blue sky. She crossed to the barrier and looked up. Out there, perhaps, was the star she had come from, uncounted millennia ago. It was possible, she thought, that between her sleeping and waking the whole vast wheel of the galaxy had made a quarter-turn in its silent revolution. How many of her siblings had survived she could not know; probably none, unless the universe was richer than they had imagined. She herself had had the greatest possible luck: she had wakened among an intelligent, technically skilled, and highly sensitive race whose culture and psychology were a puzzle that could occupy her happily for centuries.

There were many things she did not yet understand. She knew that she was aboard a floating construction adrift, for reasons incomprehensible to her, on an enormous ocean of water, but she also knew that human beings were a land-dwelling race, with many great cities on the continents and islands of this world, and that Sea Venture was intended to land at a place called Guam, and then at another place called Manila, which she visualized as sunny and green.

She turned, and saw someone coming toward her along the deck: it was a man, young, with a silly soft cap on his head. His hands were in his pockets. As he came nearer, she saw that he had a weak pale face.

"Good evening," he said, touching the visor of his cap. He was dressed in dungarees, much faded and patched, in the style of a generation ago; there was a flowered scarf at his neck. He looked anything but dangerous; he was about to pass on, but she said, "Can you tell me what time it is?"

He stopped and looked at his ring watch. "It's three-fourteen. Pretty late. Can't sleep, huh?"

"No. That is—I have a problem."

He came a step closer. "What's the problem?"

She tried to smile. "No place to sleep. I—had a quarrel with my husband."

"Oh." He peered at her face. "Aren't you—I saw the squib on the p.a.—Mrs. Claiborne?"

"Yes. Please don't tell you saw me."

"Okay, but your husband—won't he be pretty worried?"

"I can't go back there. Tomorrow, maybe, when he's had time to cool down . . ."

"Would he hurt you?" His face had turned anxious and sympathetic.

"He might."

"Well, look—" In the dim light she could see him flushing with embarrassment. "If you wouldn't mind—you could sleep in my room if you want. I mean, I stay up all night sometimes."

"That's very generous of you, Mr.—"

"Norm Yeager." He put out his hand awkwardly, and she took it. He pulled it away again a moment later, as if she had burned him. That was interesting; he seemed to be thinking of copulatory behavior and yet not to desire it.

"Well, then, if it's okay?"

"I am awfully sleepy."

His room was on the Promenade Deck near the bow. When he opened the door for her, the lights came on and music began to play. "I'll turn that off," he said hastily.

"No, I like it. It's Boccherini, isn't it?"

"You know music? That's great." He looked around the little room, darted at the bed and swept up a pile of magazines. "Uh, can I get you anything? Are you hungry?"

"No, I just want to sleep." She pulled back the coverlet, kicked her shoes off, and lay down. "Thank you very much," she said, and closed her eyes. She felt the blackness welling up, and let it come.

The man leaned over to listen to her breathing. She was asleep already, he thought. He went to his relaxer and sat down. He had never had a woman in his room before, not like this, and it was exciting and dangerous. He felt that he had done something noble and strong; he loved her for accepting his protection, and he was glad that she was asleep so that he didn't have to talk to her.

His name was Norman Peale Yeager; at twenty-five, he was in charge of Sea Venture's two independent computer systems, not in name but in fact; his boss, Dan Jacobs, attended the staff meetings, made out the reports, and gave Yeager orders, but it was Yeager who knew the systems through and through, and Yeager who had to fix them if anything went wrong. He did a few hours of maintenance a week, and he was on call twenty-four hours a day, but most of his time was his own, and that was the way he liked it.

On his shelves he had dozens of old LPs, silky plastic discs whose almost invisible spirals gleamed iridescent when he tilted them to the light, and he had a lovingly restored 1982 stereo to play them on. In the evenings, alone in the lamplight, he played them over and over, loving the rich sounds hiding behind the hiss and crackle like music from the past filtering up through layers of time.

Even older things obsessed him; he liked tales of dragons

and heroes, of fair maidens carried fainting over saddlebows, of caves and quests and treasures. He daydreamed of living in a higher and nobler age, when a man could fight for good against evil and could triumph in victory or make himself immortal in defeat. Everything that was modern seemed to him an offense: the clothes people wore, the way they talked and moved, the blemishes on their skin. It seemed to him that some apocalypse must come, to burn and wash away the grimy world he knew.

He turned the music down and dozed in his chair. In the morning, not wanting the steward to see who was in his bed, he went out for breakfast. A little after noon, when he came back, he saw that the maid had been in the room, but Mrs. Claiborne was still asleep. About two o'clock he tried to waken her, and it was only then that he realized that it was not sleep but something else.

21

On Tuesday Bliss invited McNulty to attend the weekly staff meeting in his office. Present, besides Bliss, were Armand Schaffer, the head of food services, Pete Williams, the maintenance chief, Arline Truman, passenger services, Walter Taggart, engineering, Dan Jacobs, electronics, Charles Skolnik, chief steward, and Erik Seaver, purser.

Bliss introduced McNulty and said, "Before we do our usual Tuesday drill, I'd like to discuss the problems we're having as a result of the epidemic, if I can call it that. Mr. Skolnik, will you begin? You must be getting most of the complaints."

Skolnik smiled faintly. "When they can't get us, they dump on Arline. We're running about three hours behind on room service, and it's getting worse. I'd say probably about seventy percent of the passengers are taking all their meals in

111

their rooms. We're doing our best, but we were never set up for that.''

"Mr. Schaffer, does that figure conform to your experience?"

"Our restaurant attendance is down almost eighty percent. Most of my people are working for Skolnik now."

"Ms. Truman?"

"Charles is right, we're spending most of our time trying to calm down people who can't get room service on the phone. It's a very unpleasant situation."

"Some of these people are practically barricading themselves in their rooms," Skolnik said. "When the steward knocks on their door, they holler to leave the cart and go away. It's a morale problem for us, because we have to bill them for those meals, and the stewards don't get their tips."

"Any suggestions?" Bliss asked.

"I think we ought to consider a bonus to the stewards, to come out of general funds. Say fifteen percent of their pay."

"I agree," said Truman. "The stewards are carrying the whole load—if they get really unhappy, we're all in trouble."

"Fifteen percent is too much," said Seaver.

"No, it really isn't," Skolnik answered. "In fact, it's on the low side, because we're talking about fifteen percent of their base salary, which is only about a third of their income. If they were delivering meals the usual way, they'd be getting fifteen percent and more on the charge for the food. I'd say definitely it ought to be at least fifteen, and I'd appreciate it if you'd come down and make the announcement yourself, Mr. Bliss, and, you know, thank them for what they're doing under these trying circumstances and so on."

"Mr. Seaver, is that agreeable to you?"

Seaver shrugged. "Okay."

"All right, then." Bliss made a note. "Now about passenger morale—I think that's the major problem, isn't it? Any ideas?"

"If we could tell them something reassuring about the epidemic—" said Truman.

"Any prospect of that, Dr. McNulty?"

"None that I can see. We're still getting five or six cases a day."

"Even though people are hiding in their rooms?" Truman asked.

"Yes."

"Could we do something to convince them that they're just as safe if they come out?"

"No, because it wouldn't be true. Some people are being infected in their rooms—from stewards usually—but most of them are getting it in public places."

"Dr. McNulty, that brings up the issue of asking people to report to you if they feel faint. Shouldn't we be doing that with the stewards, at least?"

"All I can say is it didn't work before. Five or six a day is bad enough, but we were getting nine and ten."

"I just don't understand that," said Truman. "How could something like that make the disease spread faster?"

McNulty hesitated. "Let me tell you, I don't understand it either. Ordinarily, if you've got a communicable disease, either it spreads broadcast, through the air, or drinking water, or some vector like an insect, or else it spreads by contact. Either way, you get a rising curve of infection until it levels off somewhere. This isn't like that. What we're seeing is one case at a time. The only way it makes sense is if there *is* a

113

vector, like a bug, say, but just one single bug. Think of some little insect that's a carrier of the disease—it gets on you, you get sick, then it jumps off and gets on me, I get sick, and so on.''

"Have you found anything like that on the patients?''

"No. But remember, there's a latent period after the infection is passed on. By the time we see the patient, they've already infected somebody else.''

"So if we could examine somebody while they're latent—?''

"That was the idea, but we never could do it.''

Skolnik said, "Dr. McNulty, does it sound to you like this is a smart bug?''

McNulty did not smile. "That's a thought that's crossed my mind.''

"Are you serious?''

"I don't know if I am or not.''

"Well, if you don't know, who does?''

Bliss rapped gently on the table. "Gentlemen, and Ms. Truman, we're all under a strain. Dr. McNulty is doing his best, and I know we're all grateful to him.''

"Let's talk about this a little more,'' said Truman after a moment. "Doctor, is it conceivable that this isn't an epidemic at all? Could somebody be going around squirting people with something, or injecting them with some poison?''

There was a stir around the table. "My God, what a horrible idea,'' somebody said.

"I don't see how it's possible,'' McNulty answered. "It can't be one person, because there's no one person that's always there. Often there's nobody around but the two people— the one that's infected, and the one they pass it on to.''

"Could it be on something that they hand each other—a coin, for instance?"

"No. Usually there's no contact."

Bliss sighed. "Now, Doctor, is it the fact that nobody you've consulted has been able to throw any light?"

"Yes."

"And we can't say when, if ever, we'll be able to stop this thing?"

"True."

Arline Truman leaned forward. "You said that sometimes there are only two people in a room when it happens. Wouldn't that be our best chance? This may sound heartless, but suppose instead of sending somebody to pick up the person who's ill, we send a nurse in there to take care of them and just keep the room locked?"

"Then you've got three people in there," McNulty said wearily. "What do you do when all three of them get sick? Send in a fourth one—who has to be a nurse? Before the day was out, you'd have the room packed with nurses, all sick but one. The infection rate wouldn't go down, the only difference would be that we'd be losing nurses, and we can't spare them."

"Are there other suggestions?" asked Bliss. He waited. "I hope we'll all be thinking about this before we meet again. Meanwhile, let's get on to other matters and let Dr. McNulty go back to his patients."

Early on the tenth day, about nine o'clock, one of the volunteer nurses came running in. "Dr. McNulty, one of my patients looks better. I think he tried to say something."

The patient was Randall Geller. He looked disoriented, but

115

his eyes were focusing. His lips moved when McNulty bent over. ''Wha' happened?''

''You've been very ill, Mr. Geller, but you're better now.'' McNulty took Geller's pulse; it was a little stronger.

Late that afternoon Yvonne Barlow regained consciousness. By that time Geller was feeling strong enough to be helped to the bathroom. McNulty called Bliss and said, ''I think we're out of the woods.''

It was a wonderful feeling, but it was premature.

22

By Monday Randall Geller was sitting up, looking feeble but alert. McNulty asked him, "What do you remember about getting sick?"

"Not a thing. The last I remember, I was talking to Yvonne."

"What were you talking about?"

"I don't know, nothing much. Just talking."

"What about before then? Do you remember any momentary faintness, for instance?"

Geller looked thoughtful. "Well, yeah. The day before. Just for a second, I felt like I was going to fall down."

"What were you doing at the time?"

"I was talking to that visiting fireman. What's his name, Newland."

"What about?"

"Well, I was showing him some manganese nodules we

117

dredged up. There was an australite in one of them—a kind of glass meteorite. Pretty unusual.''

''A glass meteorite,'' said McNulty, scribbling a note. ''Never heard of that one. What do they look like?''

''This one was hollow, about a centimeter across.''

''Don't suppose anything could have got out of it to make you sick,'' said McNulty, attempting a joke.

''Well, it could. I cracked it open.''

McNulty stared at him. ''Where is it now?''

''I gave it to Yvonne. I guess she put it away somewhere.''

McNulty went and talked to Ms. Barlow. She was recovering a little faster than Geller had; there were deep semicircles under her eyes, but her color was good.

''Ms. Barlow, if you're feeling up to it, I'd like to ask you some questions. Do you remember anything about when you collapsed?''

''No. I was in the dredge room, and somebody called in that the lunch cart was here. And that's the last I remember until I woke up in the hospital.''

McNulty made a note. ''Mr. Geller was telling me about this thing he found in a manganese nodule—some kind of meteorite?''

''Yes, an australite.''

''What did you do with it, do you remember?''

''I labeled it and put it in a cabinet in my office.''

''If I call somebody down there, could you tell them where it is and get them to bring it up?''

''Sure. Call Tim Vincent. What do you want it for?''

''I'm not sure yet.''

McNulty got Vincent on the phone and handed it to her.

"Tim, in the right-hand cabinet on the wall across from my desk, on the second shelf there's a labeled australite—the one Randy found in the nodule. Could you find it and bring it up to Dr. McNulty?" She handed back the phone. "He'll be up in a few minutes."

Vincent was a narrow-faced young man with an uneasy smile. "This what you wanted?" he asked.

McNulty took the cracked sphere and turned it over in his fingers. "Guess so. Is this the way they usually look?"

"They come in all kinds of shapes. Some are like little flat buttons. Some are lumps."

McNulty sniffed at it. "Could you analyze the inside of this to see if anything was in it?"

"What would I be testing for?"

"Damn if I know. Some kind of gas, maybe."

"Well, that's a big order. If it was a gas, there wouldn't be anything left in there, anyway."

"Volatile oil, then? See what you can do, will you? I'd really appreciate it."

"Okay," said Vincent without visible enthusiasm, and went away.

The next day he found Geller sitting up and eating poached eggs and toast with apparent appetite. "Feeling pretty good?" he asked.

"Sure. Raring to go."

McNulty sat down and looked at his chart. In fact, Geller seemed to be making a remarkable recovery.

"We were talking before about your dizzy spell when you opened the australite. Do you think there could be some connection between that and your getting sick?"

"That's *post hoc, ergo propter hoc*," Geller said with his mouth full.

"I'm sorry?"

Geller swallowed. "After which, therefore because of which. A common logical fallacy. Before you can show a causal connection, you have to exclude sources of error. In other words, did anything else happen besides opening the australite that could have started the epidemic?"

"Such as what?"

"I don't know. It's all bullshit, anyway."

"What do you mean?" McNulty asked. There was a funny expression on Geller's face.

"Ah, hell. That's just the conventional crap I was feeding you. I don't even know why I said it. Sure, I think something came out of that australite. I'll tell you something else, I think it's intelligent."

"But you say you didn't see anything when you cracked the thing open?"

"Right. So it's invisible, or it's a gas, or too small to be seen, or some kind of coherent packet of energy, or who knows what. One thing we can be pretty sure of, it's not from here. It fell out of space, maybe millions of years ago. So there's no reason to expect it to look like anything we're familiar with."

"I've been thinking the same thing, but I thought I was crazy. The damn thing knows what we're doing. When I asked people to come in if they felt faint, it jumped from one to another every time they started to do it. All right, suppose all this is true. What can we do about it? Give me some ideas—I'm fresh out."

Geller leaned back and wiped his lips, looking pleased.

120

"Well, what do we know so far? First of all, we know that the collapse comes when the thing leaves. When it goes into somebody, they feel faint for a minute. Second, we know, or at least I know, that it doesn't make you feel any different while it's in you."

"What about afterward?" McNulty asked delicately. "Do you feel different now?"

Geller scowled at him. "I don't know. Maybe. There's your *post hoc, ergo propter hoc* again. If I do feel different, we still don't know if it's because I had the parasite."

"Could you tell me what the difference is?"

"In how I feel?" Geller hesitated. "To tell you the truth, I'm just not buying a lot of the stuff I used to swallow."

"That could happen to anybody," McNulty said sympathetically.

"Sure. So let's skip it and get back to the parasite. One thing we know, it couldn't get out of that glass ball until it was broken. So whatever it is, it probably can't pass through a solid object. So the problem is to get the jinni back in the bottle."

McNulty had his notepad out and was doodling. "If we put somebody in a glass case?" he said tentatively.

"It's too smart for that. Unless we could get them when they're asleep."

McNulty shook his head. "Glass case," he said. "Like an aquarium? What would you do about the seams? There'd have to be an air supply. Might get out through the hoses. Got to be something better."

"Well, what are its limitations? First of all, it never has gone through a wall or anything, as far as we know—is that right?"

121

McNulty nodded.

"Okay, that's something. Next thing, how far away have the patients been from each other?"

McNulty looked startled. "Never thought of that. They've all been close."

"What's the farthest?"

"I'd have to ask. Probably three, four feet."

"Okay, if it never has gone farther than that, it may be because it can't. Anything else?"

McNulty stared at the wall. "Sleep," he said. "You talked about sleep. I'd have to go through the interviews, but I bet I'm right—it never has left a person when they were asleep."

"Good. All right, let's see what we've got. It can't go through walls, it can't travel more than three or four feet between people, and it can't leave a sleeping person. What does that add up to?"

McNulty looked at the desk awhile. "What it adds up to," he said, "is who's going to bell the cat?"

23

Three or four people popped out of their offices to greet him as he walked down the hall. "Glad to see you back," they said, with embarrassed smiles. "You okay now? That's great."

"Listen, I'm *really* glad to see you back," said Tim Vincent. The cigarette in his mouth was trembling. "We've been terrifically shorthanded here since you and Yvonne got sick. If you can start doing the temp and salinity again, and all that stuff, it'll really make a difference."

"Sure," said Geller.

"Well—it's about time for the ten o'clock. Can you take over now? Is it okay?"

"I said so, didn't I?"

"All right. Sorry. See you later." Vincent disappeared into his lab.

Geller looked at the familiar instruments; it was amazing

123

that he had never noticed how ugly they were. He picked up the log, looked over the last few entries in Vincent's crummy handwriting. Feeling an unreasonable irritation, he checked the recording salinometer and thermometer, put them back through the hatch and started them down on the cable. It was time for the dredge too; he noticed in the log that Vincent had skipped that a few times. Too busy dissecting his fish. He started the dredge cable, noted the time in the log, and poured himself a cup of coffee.

Water samples were lined up in a rack, about a week's worth, labeled with date, time and depth, but the analyses had not been done. It would take him at least a week to catch up, working a couple of hours overtime every day.

He picked up the first one, took a measured sample, added reagents. PCB, twenty-one parts per million. He noted it on a fresh page in the log. What was he doing this for?

He sat down and tried to remember how he had felt about his work before he got sick. It had never been any more fun than it was now, as far as he could recall, but he had done it anyway, one day after the next: why was that? Gathering data—grim little numbers in a book. He remembered something he had told Newland—"I'm not that crazy about theories. What we need is data." Balls. The data went into computers, and the computers drew charts and graphs, piling up ugly stacks of paper, and eventually somebody would analyze them and come up with some new revision of a revision of the model of deep-water distribution.

With startling clarity, he suddenly remembered the experience that had made him go into marine science in the first place. He was sixteen, a high-school kid in Skokie, Illinois. It was a warm May day, and the windows were open in the biology room, the fresh air blowing in to mingle with the stinks. Some visiting scientist was there, a skinny guy with receding ginger-colored hair. Geller couldn't even remember his name. He wasn't paying much attention until the guy showed them a little bottle with a cork in it and a yellowed slip of paper inside. He handed it around for them to look at, and when it came to Geller, he read the violet writing on the paper through the bluish glass, spidery, faded, almost invisible: *San Francisco, July 17, 1893*. And he heard the ginger-haired man saying, "That bottle was picked up by a Japanese fisherman off Hokkaido in January, nineteen sixty-three."

Seventy years. And right then, with the image in his head of that bottle bobbing around and around the Pacific current since before his parents were born, he knew what he wanted to do with his life.

Then college, and the M.S., and the goddamn dissertation, garbage done the way his professor wanted it. He had known it would be hard work, and he had realized the importance of objectivity. You could not afford to let your romantic feelings get in the way: you had to look at the instruments. One Sunday afternoon, about six months after he came to Sea Venture, he was on the Sports Deck looking out through the screen, and he realized suddenly that he hated the sight of the ocean. He never went up there again, and on his next vacation he went as far inland as he could get.

He had told McNulty that he wasn't buying the stuff he used to swallow, and that was true, but it was more than that. He felt now that he had been supremely, unbelievably dumb for the last ten years.

He looked at the racks of water samples, then got up and took off his lab coat.

Vincent came out of his lab as he passed the fish tanks. "Everything okay?" he asked.

"Sure."

"Where you going now?"

"Out. If you see Yvonne, tell her I quit."

Vincent followed him down the hall. "Randy, are you still sick?"

"Hell, no, I'm feeling fine, but this is a dumb job and they can shove it."

"Now wait a minute." Vincent caught up to him and grabbed him by the sleeve. "Are you telling me you're going to walk out and leave me to do my work and yours too?"

"Take your hand off me, you stupid bastard."

"What? Listen, Geller, I've taken about enough—"

Geller hit him in the mouth as hard as he could. Vincent went sprawling on the floor. When he got up, Geller hit him again; this time he stayed down.

24

There it came, down the long corridor, crickety, crickety, crickety. Emily stopped, turned her head to listen.

"What's the matter now?" said Jim.

"Don't you hear it?"

"Hear what?"

"The grocery cart." It was coming nearer, crickety, crickety.

Jim took her arm. "What are you talking about, for God's sake?"

"It's his grocery cart." A tall, sour-smelling man was coming toward them down the corridor; the sound trailed behind him, ghostly, echoing. The man turned and went down a side corridor, and the sound went with him. Emily started to follow, but Jim was holding her arm.

"Whose grocery cart?"

"Danny's. He's here, he wants to tell us something."

"Oh, Christ," said Jim. He looked as if he were about to cry.

*   *   *

McNulty walked into the room where his patient was waiting, introduced himself, shook hands and sat down with his elbows on the desk. "You say it's about your wife, Mr. Woodruff?"

Woodruff was in his mid-sixties, red-faced and white-haired; he looked like a man who had been prosperous most of his life, but there was something wrong with the look in his eyes. McNulty had seen that look before, in the eyes of people who had gone through some shattering loss: it was a wounded look, hard to describe—the scleras a little darkened, maybe, a pinched expression in the eyelids.

"She's hearing things," Woodruff said. He was holding onto one hand with the other, hard enough to make the fingers turn red and yellow.

"What kind of things does she hear?"

Woodruff swallowed. "A grocery cart. She hears a grocery cart coming down the hall behind some guy, and then she wants to follow him."

"How many times has this happened?"

"Twice. The first time was yesterday. Then she heard it again this morning when we were on our way to breakfast, and she followed this same guy into the restaurant. Then we ordered, and halfway through breakfast, this guy fell over out of his chair."

McNulty perked up. "Where was this?"

"In the Madison Restaurant, where we always eat."

"About nine-thirty, was it?"

"Yeah, about that."

McNulty doodled a big check mark on his pad. "That's interesting. Then what?"

128

"Then she heard the noise again when somebody else got up from another table. A woman. And she got up too and followed her out. I had to talk her out of getting in the elevator. I took her back to the room and made her take a pill."

"What kind of medication is she on?"

"Valium, and some other stuff for sleeping pills, I forget what it is."

McNulty made another doodle, a spiral this time. "Has she ever had any mental disturbance before?"

"Yeah," said Woodruff, and looked down at his hands. "She had a nervous breakdown after our boy died in seventy-three. She was in the hospital for five months."

"What kind of treatment did she get there, do you know?"

"Insulin."

"Insulin shock?"

"Yes."

"Surprised to hear that," McNulty said, and looked at his doodles. "What about afterwards—did she ever hear things until now?"

"No. She's always been nervous. She's a nervous woman."

"Now," McNulty said, "what about the grocery cart? That seems like a funny thing to hear. Does it mean anything to you?"

Woodruff did not answer for a moment. When McNulty looked at him, tears were spilling over his eyelids. "Yeah," he said hoarsely. "Yeah. It was Danny."

Danny was their youngest, born when Emily was thirty-five. When the boy was about two years old, Jim found an abandoned grocery cart in a weedy lot down the street. There

129

was nothing on it to show where it belonged, so he brought it home just to keep it from being an eyesore. He thought he might give it to the handyman, or something, but when Danny saw it, he claimed it for his own. It was his favorite toy. There was something wrong with the wheels; they made a cricking sound when he pushed it, around and around through the house. "At least you always know where he is," Jim had said.

That summer of 1973 Jim had bought a big new motor home, and it was all packed for their vacation. A neighbor, Walt Singleton, was standing at the end of the driveway to help Jim when he backed the motor home out of the garage. Emily had gone into the house to get some last-minute thing, and he had tired of waiting for her. He remembered the new-leather smell of the upholstery, the brightness of the sunlight through the blue-tinted windshield. He remembered starting the engine and listening to its confident purr. Watching Walt in the rearview mirror, he put the gearshift into reverse and drifted slowly backward. Then he felt a bump, and heard Walt scream.

"Doc, that was twenty-five years ago," he said. "What the hell, can't we ever—" His voice broke.

25

Two weeks after the horror began, panic was growing in Sea Venture. Instead of going to restaurants for their meals, many people made forays on the kitchens, grabbed whatever food they could, and carried it back to their rooms. Sometimes other passengers took it away from them in the corridors. The reckless few who spent their time in public places were becoming more violent and unpredictable. The casino had to shut down after a series of free-for-alls; nearly all the shops and most of the restaurants were closed. Vandalism was becoming a problem; deck chairs and equipment were hurled about on the Sports Deck; light fixtures in the ceilings were broken.

At one of the staff meetings, now being held daily, they talked about the food problem.

"Let's set up food-distribution stations in the lobbies," suggested Arline Truman. "Just a line of tables—let people

131

take what they want. Maybe it'll be more orderly if they know we think it's all right to take the food."

"They'll hoard it," said Armand Schaffer.

"Well, perhaps, but then they won't have to come back every day."

"That means a lot of wastage. What if we do it this way—make up cartons of staple food, either cans or the kind of thing that will keep in refrigerators. Try to get some kind of nutritional balance. Buffet food. Ham, cold chicken, roast beef. They can survive on that awhile. Then you don't have them grabbing for this and that. I agree that would be a mess."

"What about deliveries to people who can't get out so easily?"

"We can handle that," Skolnik said. "I'm a little more worried about sanitation. Those rooms must be getting filthy— the maids can't get in. We're trying to keep up deliveries of clean sheets and towels and so on, but we're shorthanded even for that. What if we get another outbreak of disease here? That would really put the capper on it."

Luis Padilla wheeled his cart up to the door of 18 and knocked. "Just a minute," came a slurred voice.

The door opened and Mrs. Emerton stood there, swaying a little. "Oh, it's Luis," she said. Her eyes did not quite focus. "Luis is back, isn't that nice, David? Come in, Luis. Look, David, it's Luis."

She stumbled as she walked ahead of him. She was wearing a negligee, a blue one through which he could see the gleam of her enormous buttocks. Mr. Emerton, with a glassy smile, was sprawled on the divan with his necktie hanging.

CV

Mrs. Emerton made an elephantine turn, tipped and sat down heavily beside him. "Put there," she mumbled. "Luis."

Padilla moved the highball glasses aside and unloaded his cart: caviar, of course, crackers, a split of champagne. Mr. Emerton's eyes were closed; he had slipped a little farther down the sofa. Mrs. Emerton mumbled something else; then her eyes closed and her mouth fell open. Mr. Emerton was snoring.

Beyond her, on the dressing table, he could see the open jewel box with necklaces scattered beside it.

"Mrs. Emerton?" he said, leaning over. She did not answer.

Padilla walked silently around the end of the divan and looked at the jewels. The emerald alone was probably worth fifty thousand dollars. In the jewel case was a star-sapphire ring, almost as big. The pearls were certainly genuine. Padilla picked them up and slipped them into his pocket, then the emerald and the sapphire, then two diamond clips and a solitaire. Together they might bring seventy or eighty thousand dollars in Manila; his cousin Renaldo would know how to dispose of them. With this and his savings, he could buy the home for his father's retirement now.

He tiptoed back to the table, replaced the things he had brought on his cart, moved the highball glasses to their former positions.

Outside in the corridor, he left the cart beside the door. If he said he had knocked and no one answered, they would remember nothing when they woke up. In the service elevator, he began to whistle.

26

When Stevens found out that Professor Newland was convalescing in the room next to his, he was sufficiently amused to drop in and introduce himself. By comparing notes, they discovered that they had been stricken within a few minutes of each other. The infection had passed from Stevens to a woman in the elevator, from her to the steward Kim Lee, and from Kim to Newland. "It almost makes you think there's some meaningful connection, doesn't it?" Newland said.

"As if we were intended to meet?" Stevens said. "I should have preferred some other way."

Newland smiled. "Well, I would too, but we don't always get to choose. Don't you feel, when you look back at your life, that everything important has been the result of some accident?"

"No," said Stevens. "I don't believe in accidents."

It had crossed his mind, in fact, that there might be

nothing accidental about the epidemic; that it might be the work of the group that employed him; certainly, if he had identified them correctly, nothing could have been more apt to their purpose. But if they had planned such a thing, his employment would not have been necessary and he would not be here.

He had wondered, too, whether there was any point now in the assassination he had been paid to carry out. Again assuming that he knew his employers' motives, surely Newland's death would go almost unnoticed in the general catastrophe and would serve no purpose. But he was not paid to speculate. He had received no new instructions, and did not expect any.

More to the point, he no longer knew what he wanted. He found that he rather liked Newland; under other circumstances it would have been a pleasure to cultivate his friendship. It amused him to contemplate the fact that Newland's life hung on an essentially whimsical decision which he had yet to make.

For the first time in many years, he was curious about his own motives. For the fanatics and tyrants who employed him he had nothing but contempt. He had never killed out of passion or conviction. Professionalism aside, he killed in order to confront death by giving it.

Now he had begun to wonder if his attitudes and beliefs were merely the chemical residues of early experiences in his brain, like those of other men. Would he have been different if his father had not killed himself, in a dirty Paris hotel, when Stevens was thirteen? Or if his childhood lover, Maria Talliavera, had not been killed by her stepfather in the attic of the house on the rue des Jardins? Was there another

Stevens who might have existed, might still exist, crying inside like an unborn twin?

The talk turned to L-5 and then to Sea Venture. "I can see all the obvious similarities," Newland said. "They're striking, and they were very effective on Capitol Hill. Sea Venture is the prototype of a self-sufficient habitat in a partly explored element; it has some of the same technical problems—integrity of the hull, life support, communications, airlocks, and so on. Even some of the solutions are the same."

"Then, do you think it makes sense to go into the oceans instead of into outer space?" Stevens asked politely.

"If we can't do both?" Newland said. "I honestly don't know. I suppose it depends on what you want. One of the great attractions of L-Five was always that it meant going into an absolutely alien medium, a place where humankind had *never* been. Extending our range, not by just a few million square miles, but almost indefinitely. That had a very powerful appeal. But I'm not sure anymore why we do what we do."

"Or whether it is a good thing for human beings to exist?"

Newland glanced at him curiously. "That's something I hadn't given much thought to. I suppose we take it as a given."

"But not for any logical reason?"

"No, not a logical reason. Do you hate the human race, John?"

"Oh, no. Schopenhauer said that to hate every miserable creature one meets would take all one's time, whereas one can despise them with perfect ease."

"I see." Newland stroked his chin. "And that's your philosophy?"

137

"Like you, I'm not sure anymore what my philosophy is. At one time I thought it was enough to be aware of the absurdity of the human animal, to eat well, sleep well, and have a healthy conscience."

"And how do you manage that?"

"I don't anymore. A healthy conscience, I must tell you, is like a healthy liver—when it is healthy, it doesn't bother you. But that was when I was thirty-nine."

"How old are you now?"

"I was forty three days ago."

"A great age," said Newland gravely.

Stevens grinned. "*Touché*. And you, Paul, how old are you?"

"I'm sixty-three. For what it's worth, I've been through four of these age things. The first one was when I was a little over thirty. I thought, here I am, thirty-one or thirty-two, my life is half over, and what have I done?"

"Yes."

"And then again in my forties, and fifties. And the sixties. It's the numbers; they're like the numbers on an odometer: every time the big one changes, it calls your attention to the time that's gone."

Stevens was watching him intently. "Do you ever think it would be better just to have done with it?"

"Oh." Newland looked at his hands. "No, not seriously. There's always been something more to do, and I've always known that when you get out of one of these troughs, things look bright again."

"Darkest before the dawn," said Stevens, not quite keeping the irony out of his voice.

138

CV

Newland folded his hands. "All I can tell you," he said, "is that I still have a strong sense of some meaning in life, even if I can't say what it is. We all have to decide for ourselves whether that's enough. Give yourself a chance."

27

His first meeting with Julie and her parents after their recovery was a subdued occasion. They had lunch in the Prescotts' suite—ham sandwiches and tea. Prescott went out for supplies every other day; except for that, they did not venture out of their room, and Mrs. Prescott, although she tried to seem gay, was obviously in a state bordering on hysteria.

When Stevens suggested a walk on the Promenade Deck with Julie, Mrs. Prescott was horrified. "You mustn't go out there!" she said. "I forbid it, Julie."

"Mother, I've had the disease already," she said wearily.

"That doesn't matter! There are people roaming around, doing terrible things. Lionel, tell her she mustn't!"

Prescott looked embarrassed. "Julie, I really think it might be better—"

141

"I have something to talk over with John," she said. "We won't be long."

"I'll bring her back safely, Mrs. Prescott."

The Promenade Deck was almost deserted. Scraps of paper littered the carpet; the trash cans and ash receivers were overflowing. Outside, the sky was brilliant over a glittering sea.

"Let's sit down here," said Julie. Her face looked drawn. "Do you want to see me again?" she asked after a moment.

"How can you ask?" Stevens bent toward her, put a hand on her arm.

"Please." She moved away slightly. "I just want the answer. If it's yes, that's all right, and if it's no, that's all right too."

Stevens studied her curiously. There was a change in her; she was less vulnerable and somehow more interesting. He had not stopped to consider whether he really wanted her; now he discovered that he did. "Yes," he said quietly. "Let's go to my room."

Afterward she said, "It isn't the same, is it?"

"No."

"I don't love you, you know. It's better with love."

"And when did you realize that?"

"After I was sick. I didn't love you before, but I thought I did. What were you after, my parents' money? They haven't got much."

Stevens got a cigarette out of his pack and lit it. "Julie, I am not a fortune hunter."

"You're not a member of Gallard Frères in New York, either. I called a friend of Dad's."

"Did you say Gallard? It's Ballard, dear, with a *B*."

"Don't lie," she said. "What's the point of lying?"

And indeed, he could see that it was only a habit, a part of the game he had been playing so long that he had forgotten there was any other way to live.

"You know," he said, "I really wish I could tell you all the truth about myself."

She looked at him. "Do you know it all?"

"Does anyone?" He turned and put his hand on her shoulder. "Do you want us to go on meeting?"

She smiled faintly. "Yes. Why not?"

After she got well, Malcolm insisted on their leading as normal a life as possible; he could not bear the thought, he said, of keeping her cooped up in a stateroom after what she had already been through. "It's foolish to take the chance," she said. "I've had the disease, but you haven't."

"That doesn't matter," said Malcolm.

He had been frantic with worry, especially after she was found in another man's stateroom. When she explained why she had done it, he wept warm tears on her cheek. Never, he said, had any man had such a companion.

They ate in the restaurants that were still open, walked on the Promenade Deck, lounged beside the open-air pool. He was tender and solicitous, because, he said, she still hadn't got her strength back; but that was not the reason.

One day at lunch Norman Yeager came up to their table, smiling, diffident, in his worn blue jeans and his funny little hat. When she introduced them, she could tell that Malcolm, in an excess of magnanimity, was about to invite him to sit down. She warned him under the table, and after a few moments of shifting from foot to foot, Yeager went away.

"He seems perfectly harmless," Malcolm said afterward. "We could have been a little more cordial, don't you think? After all, he did you a tremendous favor. And he's probably smitten with you—why not?"

"All the more reason," she said. "Honestly, Malcolm, did you ever really think—?"

He smiled and took her hand across the table. "Only because I was out of my mind," he said.

They had met at a party in the Village. After a few words, Malcolm had gone away and come back with a bunch of grapes, which he handed to her. "I wish they were emeralds," he said.

She smiled. "That's Charles MacArthur's line."

"I know, but I mean it as much as he did. More."

Then it had all been so quick, so natural and easy. Malcolm was a lawyer, not a Perry Mason type but a sweet, gentle man. Others had told her how pretty she was, but he was the first who made her believe it. She had loved him with a pure devotion, loved him more than her life. She remembered, as if it had happened to someone else, how she had left him the moment she knew she was infected. That was reasonable, because she believed she was going to die anyway, but she had not done it because it was reasonable. If she had been able to choose between her death and his, she would have chosen unhesitatingly. That was what seemed so extraordinary to her. She still loved him, because he was dear and familiar, and loved her, but would she give up her life for his? Probably not.

That was what she had to conceal from him, the change in her, and it was more and more difficult because he knew something was wrong and would not ask.

28

On days when he had business in the passenger section, Higpen usually managed to drop in on Newland for an hour or so. Once or twice they had lunch or dinner together. Hal Winter was always present on these occasions, and sometimes a young couple, Julie Prescott and John Stevens, who had been in the hospital at the same time as Newland.

At first Higpen made allowances for their recent illness, but as time went by he grew more and more uneasy. There was something odd about all three of them; he was sure that Winter scented it too.

He told himself that part of the problem was that he simply did not care for John Stevens: he was too perfectly polite, too charming, and at the same time too ironic—the sort of young man Higpen instinctively mistrusted. He felt more sympathetic toward Julie Prescott, who seemed to be making an effort to be more cheerful than she felt. But it was the change in Newland himself that disturbed him most. Newland was as gracious as ever, his conversation as fascinating, but Higpen had the eerie impression many times that he was playing a role. Furthermore, among the three of them there seemed to be some unspoken understanding, some secret agreement that excluded both him and Hal Winter.

Once, when they were alone together for a moment, he said, "Paul, how are you feeling?"

"Very well. I'm all right."

"No aftereffects?"

"No. Not physical ones, at any rate. A philosophical fallout, maybe."

"How do you mean?"

"It's hard to explain. The other day I woke up thinking about an exchange I had with a young woman in the audience at one of my lectures. That was, oh, four or five years ago, in San Diego. I don't know why I suddenly remembered it. She stood up and asked me why I thought it was important to build cities in space, or for that matter in the ocean. We already had cities on land, she said; why not spend the money to make them better?"

He smiled at Higpen. "Well, I put her down with two or three well-chosen phrases. I said that we hadn't got where we are by settling for what we had. We've always been an exploring animal; we've gone everywhere it was possible for us to go, and done everything it was possible for us to do. That's what made us great, I said."

"Good."

"Yes, and she sat down, but the other morning I seemed to hear her voice saying, 'Why do we have to be great?' And I couldn't think of the answer."

"Well," said Higpen uncomfortably.

"You see, you can't think of it either."

Hal Winter came back into the room and sat down. "Hal, maybe you can tell us—why do we have to be great?"

Hal looked wary. "Great in what way?"

"You know, building pyramids, climbing Everest, going into space."

Hal crossed his legs. "Lots of people don't."

"No, that's true, but think where we were a hundred thousand years ago and where we are now." He turned to Higpen. "Do you remember the Tasaday?"

"In the Philippines? Yes."

"A little tribe, what was it, about twenty people, absolutely isolated in the jungle. They were still living in the Stone Age. They didn't know there were any other people in the world."

"I remember."

"And you know what? They were happy."

"They didn't know any better."

"No. They didn't. Something else I remember—it's funny how these things come back. An anthropologist once figured out that the Australian aborigines, before the white people came, had to work about ten hours a week, hunting and gathering. The rest of the time they could sit around and tell stories."

"So? They were naked savages."

"Yes, that's right. And they were *happy*. I used to know a man who had lived with the Eskimos in Alaska, and he said that in the villages where they hadn't had much contact with the white people yet, they were the happiest people he had ever known.''

"Paul, I'm not sure what you're getting at.''

"I don't know myself, but I just began to wonder, the other morning, what's wrong with being happy?''

29

On the eighteenth day, the number of patients in the hospital annex was still rising, but more slowly, and McNulty calculated that if admissions and discharges kept up at this rate, the number would level off at about thirty. He was thankful for the recoveries, but he knew no more about the illness now than he had to begin with.

There was something else: he was increasingly disturbed by the signs of personality changes he saw in the recovered patients. Geller was the first example. Anybody listening to him talk would say he was alert, intelligent, perfectly rational, and yet he had walked out of his job without any explanation and had taken a poke at a co-worker who asked him for one. That could have been just nervous fatigue, but the next day Yvonne Barlow had walked off the job too, and McNulty gathered that the marine lab was in disarray. After them on the list came two stewards. One of them, Manuel Obregón,

151

had been in some kind of trouble with his supervisor; there were charges and countercharges before the union committee. The other one, Luis Padilla, had been accused of stealing by a passenger. After Padilla there was a little string of people with exotic names, Boon Hee Koh, Jamal A. Marashi, Setsuko Nakamura, and they were sprinkled in after that, more than you would expect—as if the thing were attracted to people of unusual dress or appearance. Marashi had struck his wife during a quarrel and McNulty had to put five stitches in her lip. A Mrs. Morton Tring had left her husband of twenty years and moved in with a woman friend on the Quarter Deck. Another one had left her husband without explanation and had been found the next morning in Norman Yeager's room. There were fistfights involving recovered patients almost every day, and larger disturbances now and then. Four men, drunk and belligerent in the Quarter Deck Bar late at night, had been asked to leave by the manager; they had knocked him down, broken a bottle over his head, turned over tables, and had to be subdued by half a dozen security people. A waiter in the Madison Restaurant, asked for the second time when a customer's French toast would be ready, had said, ''Get it yourself if you're in a hurry,'' thrown a tray at the customer, walked out and had not returned.

Geller had gone back to the marine lab once since he had left, but was not there now; he did not answer his room phone or his personal phone, and it was the same with Barlow. McNulty had had them paged repeatedly; it was late afternoon before he got a call.

''This is Geller. What the fuck do you want?''

''Just want to talk to you. Do you know where Ms. Barlow is?''

"She's here. What do you want to talk about?"

"The australite, for one thing. Vincent says he doesn't know where it is—thinks you have it."

"Vincent's an idiot. Yeah, I did a little work on it with Yvonne. It isn't glass."

"No?"

"No, it's silica in microscopic cells, kind of like a blastula."

"Organic?"

"Sure, organic."

"Well, hell, then that means— Will you bring it up and let me look at it?"

"Maybe."

"I'd like to get your ideas about this thing—yours and Ms. Barlow's."

"I'll see if she wants to." Geller hung up.

Geller and Barlow wandered in about five o'clock. Both of them looked cool, relaxed and calm; there was something about the way they sat together that made McNulty think their relationship had turned personal.

"Here's the dingus," Geller said, handing over the cracked transparent sphere. "It's not an australite. Yvonne thinks it's an artifact."

"Even though it's organic?"

"It's the shape," Barlow said. "The inside of it is a perfect sphere within the limits of measurement." She handed him a record crystal; McNulty put it into the player and watched in fascination while an iridescent surface bloomed on the screen—a vast pale globe in which the lenticular cells could be made out, like some alien geodesic sphere.

"So what is it, a container, a—a kind of transportation device?"

153

"Looks like it. We break the capsule, something comes out, Randy gets sick."

"What kind of something?" McNulty asked.

"We've talked about that. Neither one of us believes in a microscopic intelligence, or an intelligent gas. Maybe it's an energy system, and that's why we can't see it. Randy thinks we ought to hunt for it with an electroscope." She grinned.

"Joke," said Geller, but he smiled too.

"Listen, something else is bothering me," said McNulty, and he told them about Emily Woodruff, the woman who thought she heard the sound of the creaking grocery cart.

He had gone to talk to Mrs. Woodruff, and had found her reasonably well-oriented; she knew the date, and who was President, and so on. She was a little loony, maybe, but no more so than a lot of his patients who were walking around, and he could not see any point in confining her; he certainly was not qualified or equipped to do any psychiatric stuff.

"Here's what I can't get out of my head," he told them. "According to her husband, Emily Woodruff followed a man who seemed to be making this grocery-cart noise into a restaurant, and then the man collapsed—that was Brian Eisenstein, one of my patients. Then she heard it again when a woman sitting nearby got up and left. And that was Mrs. Rebecca Kramer, who collapsed later that afternoon. So there you have it twice: either she can identify a person who's about to come down with the disease or else it's coincidence."

"There's a saying in the army—'Once is an accident, twice is coincidence, three times is enemy action.' I don't even think you ought to call it a disease. Call it a parasite."

"Maybe Mrs. Woodruff is your electroscope," said Barlow.

"She's getting some kind of information the rest of us aren't, and interpreting it her own way."

"What would you do if you were me?"

They looked at each other. "You first," said Geller.

"Okay," Barlow said. "The trouble is, this thing is too smart for you. If you try to grab somebody who's carrying it, it jumps to somebody else. Now suppose you could identify the host, not just when the parasite enters it but any time."

"And then what?"

"Hit him over the head with a hammer," said Geller, "cart him off to solitary. Then you've got the parasite confined to one host, and the epidemic stops."

"He's joking," said Barlow. "Not a hammer, but what about sticking him with a hypodermic? Is there something that would knock him out fast enough without killing him?"

"Sure, couple of things, but you realize what you're asking me to do?"

"Do what you want," said Geller. He belched and started to get up.

"No, wait a minute, Randy, don't be so goddamned impatient. Look, Doctor, do you want to solve your problem or not? Find the host, stick him with a hypo. Then he's unconscious and the parasite can't get out. Take him into a stateroom and leave him there, locked up, with plenty of food. When he comes to, the parasite still can't get out, because there's nobody close enough. Then you can explain over the phone."

"Would you buy that explanation, Yvonne?" Geller asked.

"I'd be madder than hell, but you can't make an omelet without breaking eggs."

"Sounds familiar. Isn't that what Himmler used to say?"

"Come on, Randy. Have you got a better idea?"

"No. How about you, Doctor?"

When they had gone, McNulty thought about them a long time. They were bright, cheerful young people, smart as whips both of them, but there was something wrong with their heads. They just didn't seem to give much of a damn. Trapping the parasite was like a game to them, and they really didn't care whether it worked or not. They hadn't even bothered to tell him their discoveries about the australite until he tracked them down. *Sociopaths*, he thought, but that wasn't it either. There was just something missing, something important, and they didn't even know it was gone.

But they were right: he couldn't think of any other answer.

30

Bliss, after waffling for two days, finally gave his permission on Tuesday. On Wednesday morning, when the first patient came in, McNulty found out where she had been stricken—it was a coffee shop down on E Deck. As soon as the patient was in bed and the tube down her nose, he called the Woodruffs and asked them to meet him in the forward lobby in E. He put on a jacket in place of his white coat, took the hypo out of the refrigerator and slipped it into his pocket. He felt like an ax murderer.

"Let's go, Lori," he said to the security woman who was waiting in the outer office with a wheelchair. "Remember, you stay behind us, and don't come up till I call you."

Emily and Jim Woodruff were sitting on a banquette in the lobby. Jim got up when he saw McNulty approaching. "I had a hard time keeping her here. She wants to go looking, she thinks it's somewhere close."

"Good," said McNulty. "Emily, are you all set?"

"Yes."

"Okay, let's just stroll around. If you hear that noise, you tell me right away."

"I'm sure he's here," she said. "Jim wouldn't let me look before."

"That's right, because we had to get everything ready."

A few people were in the lobby, looking hostile and suspicious. They glanced into the coffee shop, which was empty except for the waitress and counterman. Lori Applewhite, the security woman, was following them a few paces behind. As they reached the far side of the lobby, a man came out of the restroom. Emily's face took on a rapt expression. "There he is," she whispered.

"Him, right there?"

McNulty signaled to Applewhite, who nodded and wheeled her chair past them. The man, gray-haired and slender, was walking rapidly away. "Sir," she called.

The man turned. "Yes?"

"Security. Will you show me your ID, please?"

McNulty and the Woodruffs were walking past. "Keep on going," McNulty muttered.

The man reached into his pocket. "What's this about?"

McNulty turned, got the hypo, slipped off the cap, stuck the needle into the back of the man's neck and pressed the plunger. He yanked the hypo out again barely in time to catch the body as it fell.

Janice was waiting for them in the room at the end of the isolation corridor. They laid the man out on the bed, loosened his necktie. McNulty took the opportunity to glance into his wallet: the man's name was Roger Cooke, and he had a driver's license from Maine. He glanced up at the TV camera mounted at the corner of the ceiling. "Is that thing working?"

"Yes, Doctor."

"Okay, let's get out of here."

"I must say it seems to have worked," Bliss said. "How is he taking it?"

"He doesn't like it, but he's pretty calm. He says he's going to sue us. We're giving him priority on room service; he can get anything he wants."

"Well, that's a relief. My hat is off to you, Doctor. Have you had any thoughts about what to do with him when we get to Guam?"

"I've talked to the health commissioner there. We're trying to work something out—a coast-guard ship anchored offshore maybe. It would be better to get him to Manila. There's a lot of red tape, but I think we can put it all together. What the hell they'll do with him I don't know, but at least it'll be out of our hands."

"Thank God."

After three days Sea Venture was almost back to normal; the restaurants were full, the corridors crowded and cheerful. On the fourth day, early in the morning, McNulty got a call from the security guard who was watching Cooke's room on television. Cooke appeared to be in convulsions.

With a sinking feeling in the pit of his stomach, McNulty went there with a nurse and opened the room. The nurse was the first one to reach the patient. McNulty knelt beside her, got the man's jaw open to make sure he wasn't biting his tongue. When he looked up, the nurse was on her feet, swaying a little. She took two steps toward the door, then fell like a tree. Before he could call out, McNulty heard another body fall in the corridor.

Cooke was dead; there was a line of victims in the hall. The horror had escaped.

31

McNulty finished out his workday, went home, took a couple of Nembutals and went to sleep. He woke up in the morning with the clear recollection of what had happened and the knowledge that he could no longer call himself fit to practice medicine. He had broken the oldest rule in the book: "The regimen I adopt shall be for the benefit of my patients according to my ability and judgment, and not for their hurt or any wrong."

He discovered that the knowledge of his guilt was only what he had always suspected. If this had been Santa Barbara, he could have walked out the door, but it wasn't. For better or worse, McNulty was the only medical doctor on Sea Venture, and there were still things he had to do. He made up his mind that he would do them to the best of his ability—brilliantly, if possible—and then he would try to figure out what, if anything, was left of his life.

Cooke's body was on ice down in a corner of the freezer section. His family had been notified. They had been offered the option of a burial at sea, if they so desired, but they wanted the body shipped home. By rights there would be an inquiry. He was guilty of malpractice, or of murder if you looked at it that way, but the worst thing he was guilty of, the thing he could not forgive himself, was stupidity.

On the following day he began a systematic effort to locate and interview all the recovered patients. Jamal A. Marashi, the man who had struck his wife, was a Malaysian living in the United States. He seemed to McNulty an entirely selfish person; his grievances against his wife took up most of the conversation. McNulty put him down as inconclusive; for all he knew, Marashi had been exactly the same before his illness.

Luis Padilla, the steward, was another matter. At first he seemed very much at ease; he denied that he had taken any jewelry from Mr. and Mrs. Emerton, and pointed out that his record was unblemished.

"Mr. Padilla," McNulty said, "I'm a medical man, not a policeman. I don't care whether you took that stuff or not. What I'm trying to find out is, what does this disease do to people? Could you just tell me, did you feel any different after you got well? We won't talk about the jewels at all."

Padilla shifted uneasily. "Different? Well, maybe a little different."

"Could you tell me how?"

"Well, you know, how I think about things."

"Yes?"

Padilla seemed to make up his mind. "Doctor, you know, I am a Filipino. Our country was conquered by your country a hundred years ago. First your country says after they drive the Spaniards away, they will give us our independence. Then they change their minds, no, the Philippines is our country now. Our national hero, Aguinaldo, you have heard of him?''

"No," said McNulty. "I'm sorry."

Padilla smiled. "He was the leader of the independence movement. He fought many battles. The U.S. government defeated him only by treachery."

"I see," McNulty said. "So you feel differently now about Americans?"

"Not about you, Doctor," said Padilla politely. "I think you are a good man. But I know what Americans did to my country, and I think it is important for us to have pride."

"And you started thinking this way after you got well?"

"Yes." Padilla shrugged and smiled. "You want to know, why not before? I don't know why. I think maybe I listened too long to people who say, keep in your place. Remember the Americans are the boss. I don't know, but I believe the way I think now is better."

Mrs. Morton Tring turned up with the friend, Alice Gortmacher, with whom she had been staying since she left her husband. Mrs. Tring was a handsome woman in her early fifties; Ms. Gortmacher was smaller, darker and more intense. "If you *think*," she said, "you're going to get Susan to go back to that man, you're very much mistaken."

"No, no," said McNulty, "that isn't it at all. Believe me, Mrs. Tring—"

"Ms. Coleman," she said; "I'm taking my maiden name back."

"Ms. Coleman, then. I'm just interested to know if you

163

Damon Knight

experienced any change of feelings after you were ill. Did your outlook change, the way you look at things?"

"It certainly did," put in Ms. Gortmacher. "She saw for the first time what a monster she was married to."

"Is that right, Ms. Coleman?"

"Yes, well— It's not exactly that, Alice. I mean, I knew what Mort was like, but suddenly it just seemed to me that I was staying with him for all the wrong reasons."

"What sort of reasons?" McNulty asked.

"Well, you know, the usual things. The children. Mort's career. What would people say, et cetera. And then, I suppose, I was afraid, too. What would happen if I divorced Mort and went off on my own? I still don't know."

"Yes, you do," said Ms. Gortmacher, patting her hand. "*Yes*, you do."

Ms. Coleman put her hand on her friend's. "Alice is going to take me into her business," she said. "She's the dearest friend I ever had, and I don't know what I'd do without her. But even if I didn't have Alice, I'd do the same thing—I'd leave Mort."

"Can you tell me what it was that changed your mind about that?"

She hesitated. "Well, this may sound silly, but I woke up one morning, a few days after I got well, and Mort was snoring, and I just asked myself, what am I doing here? And I looked at all the reasons, and they weren't good enough. So I got up and got dressed, and called Alice, and just went."

"Ms. Coleman," said McNulty, "how many married women do you suppose there are who would feel the way you do, if they just thought it over?"

164

She glanced away for a moment. "Four out of five," she said.

"More," said Ms. Gortmacher firmly.

And, McNulty thought, she might well be right. He sympathized entirely, but what would happen to the world if the divorce rate climbed to ninety percent? If only couples who liked being together stayed together? Or if only those who knew themselves to be fitted for the practice of medicine ever became doctors?

32

Randall Geller and Yvonne Barlow, wearing dark glasses and sipping tall drinks, were lying side by side in lounge chairs near the pool, looking out across the bright ocean. Their bathing suits were almost dry. "What do you want to do next?" Barlow asked.

"Dunno. Go watch the geriatrics play shuffleboard?"

"Or sit here all day?"

"I can do with a lot of sitting here." Geller hoisted his tall glass and drank.

"Not worried about boredom?"

"Hell, no. You know what I dreamed about last night?"

"No."

"I dreamed I had the solution to the problem of sexuality."

"That sounds boring."

"It was very exciting. You know, why did bisexuality ever arise? You've got the Best Man theory, the Red Queen

167

theory, the Tangled Banks theory, and none of them work. I had it all figured out, but I forgot it."

"Maybe it was just for fun," Barlow said lazily.

"Well, why not? Pleasure is a survival factor—if it wasn't, we wouldn't have it."

"There's a circular argument if I ever heard one. Do you think a spider gets a kick from building a web?"

"No opinion," said Geller.

"Well, if you were going to design a machine to build webs, would you put pleasure into the circuit or not?"

"Oh, God."

"No, you wouldn't, because number one it wouldn't be necessary, and number two you wouldn't know how to do it, and number three if you did do it, it would be counter-productive. A spider that built webs for kicks might get bored and quit. Spiders just go ahead and build them."

"Uh-huh. You remember the elevator operator in *Brave New World*?" Geller mimicked a voice trembling with ecstasy: " 'Up, up!' " Then misery and despair: " 'Down—down!' "

"So when was the last time you saw an elevator operator?"

"Um."

They sat in peaceful silence; then Barlow said, "You ever know anybody who was rich?"

"No."

"I did—a girl I went to school with. Her parents left her umpty million dollars."

"What's her address?"

"She wouldn't look at you twice," Barlow said. "Anyway, okay, she's been married three times, she doesn't have to do a thing she doesn't want to do, and she's really a failed human being. Can you imagine life as one long birthday

168

party? She knows she blew it, and she doesn't know what to do about that, and she's very unhappy.''

"Tough," said Geller. "That's very tough."

"Sure it is. Suppose you didn't want to do anything except watch television and go to football games?''

"Paradise," said Geller.

There was a buzz from Barlow's beach bag. She reached over, extracted the phone. "Hello, Doctor."

The phone quacked at her.

"Who else would be calling us? . . . We could, but we probably won't. . . . If you want to talk, why don't you come up here? We're at the Sports Deck pool. . . . Come up if you want to." She put the phone away.

"Now why did you do that?" said Geller.

"Why not? Good for your boredom."

McNulty showed up a few minutes later, interrupting a spirited argument. "Good old Doc," said Geller. "Sit down, have a drink."

"Not during working hours, thanks," said McNulty, pulling over a web chair. "It's nice up here, isn't it? I can't remember the last time— Well, anyway, I just wanted to tell you, I've been interviewing some of the other recovered patients, and there's a pattern, all right. Marriages breaking up. People leaving their jobs. I keep thinking, maybe the parasite doesn't know what it's doing to us. If only we could talk to it."

"Well," said Barlow thoughtfully, "you know, we can. That's not the problem. Look, we're assuming the thing is intelligent and it understands what we say. So we can talk to it all we want to; the only thing is, it can't talk to us, or won't.''

"Which is it?" McNulty asked. "Randy?"

Geller shifted restlessly in his chair. "How the hell do I know?"

"While you were infected—"

"Infested," Geller muttered.

"—did you ever feel that your actions were being controlled in any way?"

"Are you kidding?" Geller got up, his face set.

"Randy," said Barlow.

"Oh, for God's sake."

"Do it for me. This is interesting. Come on."

Geller sat down sulkily. "It's all bullshit."

"What he means is, the answer is no."

"I can tell him what I mean, Yvonne."

"So tell him."

"The answer is no," said Geller. "Not just maybe or perhaps or a little bit. I know that for sure, because while I had the parasite, I did just what I would have done anyway. Look, use your brain. Here you are, you're a thing from another planet or God knows where, and you've never seen people before, or walls, or toothpicks, or coffee cups. If you could control the person you're in, what would you do? You'd walk it around and look at everything. If you could make a person talk, you'd ask questions. Then you'd have your wish."

"He means you could have a conversation with it," Barlow said. "And he's right. As far as I can tell, I didn't do or say a thing that I wouldn't have said on an ordinary day. So I think we're justified in assuming, the way we have before, that if the thing doesn't do something, it's because it can't."

170

CV

"Would you both agree," McNulty asked delicately, "that your attitudes changed after the parasite left you?"

"Sure."

"Yvonne, you too?"

"Of course. I suddenly saw I wasn't doing what I wanted to do with my life, so I quit."

"What do you want to do with your life?"

"I want to have some fun, and find out things, and do something that makes sense."

"Okay. But you know it must have been the parasite that changed your mind."

"True."

"And you like that."

"Sure, I like it."

"Don't you have to ask youself—being objective, now—if you would have liked the idea of having your mind changed, if you'd known it was going to happen?"

"That doesn't matter," Geller broke in. "Come on, you know you can't argue that one way or the other. Either we're crazy now or we were dumb before. I say we were dumb before."

"So you think the thing did you a favor?"

"A favor?" said Geller. "Maybe." He gnawed a fingernail. "Interesting question. Might be just a by-product of the parasite-host relationship. Or maybe it's a symbiote, not a parasite—it gives you something for what it gets, like the bacteria in your gut."

Barlow was nodding. "I think that's right."

"So you'd definitely say it doesn't intend us harm, basically?"

"Right."

171

"Even though it makes everything fall apart?"

"What do you mean by everything?"

"Well, the marine lab, for instance. You both walked off your jobs. What would happen if everybody walked off their jobs?"

"I don't give a damn about their stupid jobs. Look, McNulty, I know you think I'm a brainwashed idiot, but that's your problem. Take a good look at the things people do for a living and ask yourself how many of them are worth doing. How many people go through their whole goddamn lives screwing part A onto part B?"

"So you think the best thing to do would be to spread this around? Let the parasite get onto the mainland?"

"No."

McNulty glanced at Barlow, then leaned back and folded his hands. "Now, isn't there a little bit of contradiction there?"

"Think, McNulty. The system works because most people are *dumb*. That doesn't mean I have to be dumb."

"I see. And you don't feel any obligation to help make the system work? Even though you're in trouble if it doesn't?"

"No. The system will probably collapse. We'll get a new system. It might be a better one."

Next morning Emily Woodruff was wheeled into the hospital annex; she had collapsed in the Quarter Deck Breakfast Shop. McNulty looked at her and wondered if that was coincidence. Had the parasite deliberately sought her out, so they couldn't play that trick again?

33

In the name of the emergency, and with a sense of profound relief, Bliss had canceled all his formal entertainments, but the curious result was that time hung heavy on his hands in the evenings. In the ample space of his living room, intended for jolly cocktail parties of thirty or more, he felt himself isolated, almost imprisoned. He could not invite any of the VIP passengers without having to listen to their complaints all over again, and as for the staff, he saw all he wanted of them during the day. The only ones he could talk to were Dr. McNulty, who as a professional man did not exactly come under the heading of staff, and Captain Hartman, who was neither staff nor passenger.

After dinner that night in Bliss's suite, McNulty told them about his interviews with the recovered patients, particularly Geller and Barlow. "As far as I can make out," he said, "the only principle they recognize is what you might call

173

more or less enlightened self-interest. They're intelligent young people, and they're not exactly antisocial, but they just don't see the point of supporting a system they think is cockeyed.''

"And that makes you uneasy?"

"Yes, it does. Maybe the system is cockeyed, but it seems to work. I've been thinking about that lately. Lots of the things we do aren't rational. Love isn't. Having babies isn't. 'Irrational' is a dirty word, but maybe it shouldn't be. This thing, this parasite, maybe it's a completely rational being, and it just doesn't understand that human beings don't work that way. You know what they say about the road to hell?''

"No, what do they say?"

"It's paved with good intentions."

After McNulty went home, Bliss brought out the chessboard. It was his turn to play white; he used a conventional Ruy Lopez opening. Hartman played for position, as usual, but Bliss developed an unorthodox queen's-side position which turned into an ingenious combination twenty moves later. Hartman smiled when he saw it. "Well done," he said, and tipped over his king.

Afterward he accepted a whisky and said, "You know, I think the doctor is right to be worried. The other day I had a talk in a bar with two gentlemen, both recovered patients and both veterans of the Nicaraguan War. They both say quite emphatically they wouldn't do it again."

"Did you ask them," said Bliss, "what if the U.S. were invaded?"

"I did, and they said they'd fight then if they had to, because they could see some point in it. By the way, I also talked to a recovered patient who'd spent twenty years in some giant corporation or other. He said if he had it to do over, he wouldn't do that again. After he retired, he took up making stained glass, and now he says he's happy for the first time in his life.''

''That's worrisome,'' Bliss said after a moment. ''There are a good many things in life one doesn't particularly like to do; still, they've got to be done. Where would we be if everyone did just what they liked?''

''Wouldn't be any war, perhaps,'' Hartman said. ''Nobody would go and fight for democracy, or Bolshevism, or the Holy Roman Empire.''

''You have to fight sometimes.''

''Quite right, to defend home and family, but that's where your enlightened self-interest comes in. As far as I can make out, these people would fight if they were attacked, but they wouldn't attack anybody else; they would see that as a foolish risk of their own necks. I don't suppose you've read Tuchman on the Hundred Years' War?''

''Can't say that I have.''

''Well, read it sometime. You know, there was no earthly reason for that war unless you count things like wounded pride and stupidity. The French especially. They wouldn't even use archers, thought it was beneath them, and we slaughtered them at Crécy.''

''Oh, well, the French,'' said Bliss.

''We were no better, or not much. Think of the Wars of the Roses, or the Crusades.''

''Well, it's not my line, but I suppose there must have been some wars that made sense—economic sense, anyhow. Expanding markets, and so on.''

''Yes, certainly, but here you come back to the doctor's

175

enlightened self-interest again. It was in the economic interest of some people in Germany to overrun Europe twice this century, but what about the poor sods who were in the trenches getting shot? Why did they do it? Weren't they pumped up with loyalty to the Fatherland?''

"I expect so. Afraid of their sergeants, more likely."

"All right, but how many sergeants would it take to stop a platoon if they decided to go home? That's my point, you see. If it wasn't for loyalty, and these grand abstractions, you couldn't get people to fight in an ordinary war. They wouldn't let themselves be conscripted, in the first place, and if they did, you couldn't keep them from deserting."

"It goes beyond war, though, doesn't it? We all have something to be loyal to, even if it's a shipping company."

Hartman sucked on his pipe meditatively. "I worked my way up in Cunard, same as you did. Thin times we had at first. I'm thinking of a steward I knew on the old *Queen*. They demoted him to staff service for some minor offense, and he was completely devastated. It wasn't just the job to him, it was his life. There's that, and then there's getting so accustomed to a thing that you can't imagine anything else. To me the interesting question is, would there have been any shipping companies as we've known them, or any navies, if the ordinary seamen had been infected by this microbe or whatever it is? You know what Nelson said about them, that they were used up at thirty-five, half dead with scurvy, couldn't eat their rations without agonizing pain. I can't help thinking that if we'd had seamen who consulted their own interests, the whole thing would have had to be organized in quite a different way."

"All right, but are you saying that things would be better if we didn't have any nations? Or religions, or anything?"

"I'm damned if I know."

That night, as he drifted off to sleep, McNulty had a fantastic vision. It was true, he realized, that they could communicate with the parasite. All they had to do was line up some prospective victims—gagged and bound, probably—and ask the parasite yes-no questions. Take Victim Number One if it's yes, Victim Number Two if it's no. Or they could even set up an alphabet, with lettered cards on the victims' chests, like a human ouija board. After all, it would be in the interest of research.

Toward morning he dreamed that he was on his way across the lobby to his office, and the lobby was full of children. They were sitting in rings in a conversation pit, playing some incomprehensible game; he could see their bright eyes and moving lips, although he couldn't hear a sound. They were beautiful children, every one, but when he got nearer he could see that their faces were not human, and he woke up feeling as if he had been drenched in ice water. It was only a little after six, but he got up and dressed and went out into the lobby, just to make sure they were not there.

34

On Monday, at the Town Council meeting, Mrs. Bernstein said, "Item five. A complaint. Mrs. Livermore, will you state the complaint?"

Clarice Livermore stood up. "My complaint is, the Korngolds have let a couple from the passenger section move into that apartment they own at the corner of Fifth and Pacific. I didn't find out about it till they'd been here three days. That's right around the corner from our market, and it's only two blocks from the school."

"Are they disorderly people, Mrs. Livermore?"

"Well, *I* don't know, but that's not the point. They could be carrying that awful disease. Why can't they stay where they belong? I'm not the only one that feels this way," she said, and sat down.

"Mr. Korngold, do you want to respond?"

A stout gray-haired man in the audience stood up. "Mrs.

Bernstein, gentlemen, the Harrises are old friends of ours, we know them for twenty years. They're worried about the situation in the passenger section and they asked us if they could move in till the trouble is over. I don't see how that's any of Mr. and Mrs. Livermore's beeswax.''

"Well, my children's health *is* my business," cried Mrs. Livermore. "Let me tell you—"

Mrs. Bernstein rapped with her gavel. "Out of order," she said. "Mr. Korngold, do you have anything more to add?"

"No, that's it, except I think she's making a tempest out of a teapot.''

"Any discussion?"

Ira Clark leaned forward. "Mrs. Livermore, is it just these two passengers you object to, or would you like to keep everybody from the passenger section out of perm? I hope you realize that I'm the only dentist on Sea Venture, and Dr. McNulty is the only physician.''

"Well, that's one thing, but bringing in people that might be infected for no reason, that's another. That's all I say.''

Higpen caught Mrs. Bernstein's eye and said, "You know, we have about a hundred people living here and working in passenger. There's traffic back and forth every day. If we could close off perm and keep the epidemic out, I'd be for it, but we've discussed this and agreed that it isn't possible. Luckily, there hasn't been a single case in perm, and the Harrises have been here, how long?''

"Since the first of last week," said Korngold from the audience.

"Well, I'd say if they were going to infect anybody, they would have done it by now. Sorry, Clarice. I move to dismiss the complaint.''

"Further discussion?" asked Mrs. Bernstein. "All in favor."
All the Council members raised their hands. "You can step
down, Mrs. Livermore. Item six, repairs to the gymnasium."

The next day Yetta Bernstein walked into the back room of
Higpen's hardware store, where Higpen sat going over his
accounts. "Ben, let's talk."

Higpen pointed to the plastic bag on his desk. "I was just
about to have lunch."

"Bring it, we'll sit in the park. You ought to get out more
anyway."

They walked to the park, an open space the same size as
the town square. Children were running up and down the
gravel paths, playing on the jungle gym. The scent of mown
grass was sharp in the air.

"Ben, I'm worried," Bernstein said. "We've been lucky
so far, the thing has stayed in the passenger section, but how
long can we be lucky?"

"I don't know."

"I don't believe in trusting to luck. We've got to do
something."

"All right, but what?"

They sat down on a park bench, and Higpen opened his
lunch bag. "I've been thinking," Bernstein said. "The people who live here and work in passenger, maybe we could
trim that number down. Talk them into staying here till the
emergency is over. Or some of them, those that don't have
families, they could stay in passenger."

"You'll never get them all that way."

"I know it, but we might be able to reduce the traffic to
something manageable, say thirty or forty a day. Then

181

suppose—just suppose—we station people at the entrances, and every time somebody comes in, we get another person to go with them and watch them for twenty-four hours.''

"That wouldn't keep the parasite out." Higpen unwrapped a sandwich.

"No, but listen. Suppose it gets in, God forbid. All right. Then it leaves and goes to another person. The first person collapses, the second person feels faint. Now we know which person has the parasite. And we're watching. So we take that person back to passenger—maybe we tell them the truth, or maybe some cock-and-bull story—and that person doesn't get back in until the parasite jumps to somebody else.''

Higpen took a bite, chewed and swallowed. "You know," he said, "I feel two ways about this. Even if we could keep the parasite out, would it be fair? Why should the passengers take all the risk?''

"Ben, I'm ashamed of you. There are *children* here. Grown-ups can take their chances, but these kids?''

35

On Tuesday, at Bliss's invitation, Higpen and Bernstein attended the staff meeting. McNulty was also present; Geller and Barlow had been invited, but neither of them had shown up.

"Apart from the epidemic itself, I think it's fair to say that morale is our principal problem," Bliss said. "People are frightened, and some of them are behaving badly. Our head of security, Mr. Lundgren, isn't here because he can't leave the job, but speaking for him, I can say that the problem is out of hand. Our normal security staff, as you know, is only ten people. We need at least a hundred and thirty. My deputies have been working with Mr. Lundgren when they're off shift, and we've got Mr. Islip, the entertainment director, and his staff, and about fifty staff from the restaurants and the casino, but it still isn't enough; we're overworking our people and falling behind."

Higpen said, "How many volunteers do you need? What kind of duty?"

"Well, we need at least a dozen for guard, and say eighty more for patrol."

"Will they be armed?"

"That's never been necessary. We don't have firearms in Sea Venture."

"What are they supposed to do if they have to subdue somebody and arrest them?" Mrs. Bernstein wanted to know.

"Mr. Young, our chief carpenter, has provided some batons. We'd like the patrolmen to work in pairs, in three shifts around the clock. We haven't got uniforms for them, of course, but we'll give them brassards. Then we'll need about twenty-five, they could be older men, for supervisory work."

"Or women?"

"Or women, of course. Thank you, Mrs. Bernstein."

"I wasn't volunteering, although I may yet. Mr. Bliss, are you exaggerating this in any way? I can't believe you need a hundred and thirty policemen to keep order in the passenger section."

"Believe me, Mrs. Bernstein, if anything, I'm understating it. I had a delegation yesterday morning that nearly turned into a mob—some gentlemen demanding that we launch them in the lifeboats."

"You turned them down? Why not let them go and be rid of them?"

"I hope that was not a serious suggestion," said Bliss after a moment.

"Sea Venture is quarantined," said McNulty. "We can't take a chance on letting this thing spread."

"Why not, if you know it only affects one person at a

time? Lock that person up and let the rest go. Mr. Bliss, for your information, that was a serious suggestion. I'd like to know what your plans are. You tell us Sea Venture is quarantined. I assume that means we can't land at Guam. What are we going to do, just keep on going until you've lost all your passengers?''

Bliss seemed incapable of speech. McNulty said quickly, ''Mrs. Bernstein, please. We've already found out that we can't lock this thing up. What we're dealing with here isn't an ordinary infection, it's some kind of intelligent parasite.''

''I don't believe in intelligent bacteria,'' said Bernstein.

''It isn't a bacteria,'' McNulty answered. ''I don't know what it is. It's aware, it knows what we're doing, and it's outsmarted us every time. About the only thing we've got going for us is that it can't get off Sea Venture.''

''So what are you going to do?'' she demanded, looking at Bliss. ''Just keep on drifting? Why aren't we getting help from the mainland?''

Higpen cleared his throat. ''Yetta, we're getting over-wrought. Mr. Bliss is responsible for the safety of CV, and I think we have to let him do his job. There's something else, too, talking about the lifeboats. This thing is infecting, what, about six or eight people a day?''

''About that,'' said McNulty.

''Well, so far it hasn't got into the perm section. If Mr. Bliss were to evacuate the passengers in lifeboats, where would it go for its victims except to us?''

''Good point,'' said Mrs. Bernstein. ''But is there room on the lifeboats for everybody or not? Why not evacuate perms and passengers both?''

185

"Because," said Bliss, "then the parasite would be aboard one of the boats."

"All right, but at least then you'd have it confined to forty people. How about this? We announce CV is being evacuated. Everybody gets on the boats—*everybody*. Then we announce there's been a delay. And we wait until someone collapses. Then everybody from all the other boats goes back on board. What's wrong with that?"

Bliss rubbed his face wearily. "Mrs. Bernstein, it's the same as the other scheme. If we did as you suggest, presently we'd have one person taking care of thirty-nine victims— that's an impossible situation on a lifeboat. And then if we did nothing, the remaining person would go into convulsions, presumably, and we'd be back where we started."

Bernstein was doodling on her pad. After a moment she said, "We're not thinking this through. The point is, do we want to isolate the parasite or not? If we do, there's got to be a way. Dr. McNulty, you said the thing can't go from one person to another more than four or five feet away, is that right?"

"About that, apparently," McNulty said.

"So we've got two problems here. The first one is, if people collapse on the lifeboat, we can't leave them there. They've got to be taken back to the hospital."

"And the first thing the parasite would do would be to jump to one of the people who come in to get the patient," said Bliss.

"All right. So put a *rope* on a gurney or whatever you call it. Open the lifeboat door, throw the rope in. People inside put the patient on the gurney, throw the rope out. We pull the patient out and close the door. The parasite is still inside."

"That might work," McNulty said. "But then you get to the point where there's one person left, and I just don't see any way out of that. Either you go in and get that person, or else—" His voice stopped.

"That's the second problem," Mrs. Bernstein said. "But the only reason it's a problem is we're looking at it the wrong way. Why is there only one person left? Because nobody else is coming in."

"I don't quite follow," said Bliss.

"Volunteers," said Mrs. Bernstein. "Get volunteers to go into the lifeboat one at a time, whenever we take a patient out. That way there's always somebody else for the parasite to jump to, and we can keep it there, in isolation, until we figure out something else to do."

After a moment Bliss said, "By George, I think she's got it."

36

The final plan, everyone agreed, was eminently dislikable, but it was the best they could do. There had been a suggestion from Skolnik to evacuate just one deck, whichever one the parasite was known to be on; that had obvious attractions, but it quickly became clear that it was unworkable. For one thing, it would have meant new lifeboat assignments for people who happened to be on that deck at the time but were normally assigned elsewhere; for another, it would have meant closing elevators and stairways in order to keep people from wandering out of the area; and, finally, it would have been an unusual procedure which would very likely alert the parasite that something was up.

In the end they went back to the original idea, with refinements. A boat drill would be announced. In order to guard against the possibility of confining staff members on the boat that carried the parasite, they would be reassigned to passenger lifeboats. After the passengers had boarded, there would be a thorough sweep to round up any stragglers; that would take the best part of three hours, during which time the parasite, if it was on one of the boats, would probably reveal itself. At that point the sweep could be abandoned; if not, it would go on to conclusion. At the end of the procedure, everyone in the passenger section, passengers and crew alike, would be in the lifeboats except for the duty officer and Bliss himself; a skeleton crew of kitchen staff, security people and essential members of other departments; the patients in hospital; McNulty, and the current shift of nurses.

The lottery was Skolnik's idea, improved on and elaborated by Jim Islip, the entertainment director. "It isn't enough to appeal to their civic duty," he said. "Don't misunderstand me, there are a lot of good people here, and they'll volunteer. But that's *grim*, and we don't want to be grim. Let's do it this way—we'll hold a drawing every afternoon in the forward Main Deck lobby, televised all over the vessel, with cash prizes for the winners. They'll get baskets of fruit and flowers delivered to their staterooms, and we'll post their names and photographs, and publish them in the *Journal*, and believe me, we'll get more people signing up that way than we would by telling them it's their duty."

"How much cash?" Erik Seaver wanted to know.

"For these people, it'll have to be substantial or it won't mean anything. I'd say two thousand dollars for the first name drawn, fifteen hundred for the second, a thousand for the third, then five hundred apiece for all the rest."

"You're talking about seven thousand a *day*," Seaver said.

"I know it, but this isn't a time to count pennies. The

lottery has to work, and more than that, we've got to improve morale—make people see this as a kind of fun thing. If we don't, we're going to lose more than seven thousand a day just in vandalism.''

Then there was a discussion about the recovered patients. ''I see a problem here,'' McNulty said. ''So far, nobody has ever been infected twice. Now, I don't know what that means. It could mean just that the parasite has so many people to choose from, there's no reason for it to take the same host a second time. But it could mean that it can't take a person twice, because of acquired immunity, or for some other reason that we don't know.''

''What's the difference?'' Bernstein asked.

''Well, it could happen that we'll wind up with recovered patients on the lifeboat, and they'll be stuck there. We can't take them off, because we still don't know if the parasite can reinfect them or not, and if they can't get off by getting infected, how do they get off?''

''What about just excusing them from the drill in the first place?''

''I'd be afraid to risk it. If we leave them on board, and it turns out that the parasite is in one of them, we'd have to start all over.''

''We've got the same problem, only more so,'' said Schaffer, ''with the rest of the people we leave on board. My kitchen people, security, et cetera, including all of us here.''

''Let's take one problem at a time,'' Bliss said. ''About the recovered patients, Doctor, I think I see a solution. After we find out which lifeboat the parasite is aboard, we clear out all the rest. The lifeboats are in pairs, two opening from each bay. We can seal off that bay satisfactorily, I think, and then transfer any recovered patients into the next boat. As soon as the next person collapses, we'll know where we are, and then we can let the recovered patients go. Mr. Young?''

"I can run you up a good sturdy barrier," said the carpentry chief. "Put a door in it, and a lock on the door. No problem there."

"Good. Any problem with security, then, Mr. Lundgren?"

"No, with a barrier there's no reason we can't handle it."

"All right, now about the rest of us, I think that's a bit simpler. Let's agree that we'll go on drill alert at fifteen hundred hours in two days' time, but the drill won't be announced until you tell me, Doctor, that you've just had a fresh victim. If, by any bad luck, anyone on the reserve list happened to be in the same corridor or lobby as the victim, we'll make a last-minute substitution. Does that seem satisfactory to all of you? Good; then will you all please make up reserve lists, with standbys noted, and have them on my desk by oh nine hundred tomorrow?"

Really, Bliss thought afterward, he had handled that rather well. It was just possible that he was going to get through this without disgracing himself.

37

When Norman Yeager got up the next afternoon, he found
a flimsy in his tray about a new lifeboat assignment. He
knew from the number that it was a passenger lifeboat; now
why was that?

He sat down at his terminal, accessed the main computer,
and looked over the lifeboat lists; then he called Bliss's
secretary.

"Bunny, it's Norm Yeager. Why are you fooling around
with the lifeboat assignments all of a sudden, if you don't
mind my asking?"

"There's going to be a special drill," said Bunny.
"Something to do with the parasite. Keep it under your hat."

"Oh. All right." Idly he called up the lifeboat lists again
and looked at the people he was going to be with: nobody
special, and nobody he knew. Next he searched for Claiborne,
Mr. and Mrs. Malcolm. They were in Lifeboat Thirty-one.

Back to the lists, and he plucked out a name at random, M. Shanigar, and substituted his own. Then, to tidy up, he put M. Shanigar in the other lifeboat, the one where he was supposed to be. It would make a little confusion when Mr. S. got to Lifeboat Thirty-one, but never mind. At least he would get to see Mrs. Claiborne again, perhaps even to say a few words.

He really wanted no more than that, just the chance to sit down and have a talk with her, the good talk they had missed having in his room because she was so tired. He couldn't even claim that he knew her, and yet he felt that he really did: he knew the sweetness and gentleness in her, the deep enduring qualities her husband had never seen. He had watched the two of them together, after she got out of the hospital. Her husband was a gross physical presence, heavy and thick and stinking of tobacco: how could she stay with him? Sometimes he imagined her saying, "Only you can save me." And he knew that he would; he would carry her off to a mountaintop and they would live there highly and nobly, with his sword between them when they lay down at night.

And he knew at the same time that these were only imaginings, that she was a married woman with responsibilities somewhere, maybe even children; a house, friends he had never met, an occupation, the thousand details of a life. And even knowing all this, he longed for just the chance to speak to her, to hear her say, "You can help me." Because it was possible that she really wanted to get away from that man—how could she not?—and even if she only said, "Hide me," or "Please lend me some money," or anything, it would be a joy to him, yes, even if he knew he would never see her again.

CV

*　　*　　*

The boat drill took place at three-thirty. A few people were drunk in their staterooms, or elsewhere, and did not attend. There were other problems, too: the manager of the Promenade Theater had not received word, or had forgotten, and had failed to turn off his screen. Thirty people had to be rounded up from the theater, but by that time it didn't matter: the parasite had been found.

From his seat in the middle of Lifeboat Thirty-one, the fat man watched with interest as the steward called the roll. He remembered being in a lifeboat before, but he had not been paying much attention then. The lifeboat, evidently, was a small vessel which could be released from the bigger one in an emergency. Was there any possibility that an emergency would occur while he was aboard it?

"Mr. Eller?"

"Here," he answered.

The passengers opposite him were mostly prosperous-looking middle-aged Americans. There was one younger couple, holding hands, and farther down in the row there was a still younger man, unusually dressed.

The steward was explaining the features of the lifeboat and what would happen in the event of an emergency. The fat man was not looking in that direction, and could not see the control panel; hoping for a better view, he slipped out, across the fuzzy space, and in again so deftly now that she felt almost no disorientation as the fat man's weight slumped against her and then rolled to the floor.

People were standing up to look. The steward, aided by a man with a white armband, rolled the fat man over and loosened his collar. Then the steward returned to the front of the boat. "Please take your seats, ladies and gentlemen!" he called.

The lifeboat door opened and a rope flew through the opening. The steward picked it up, pulled on it; a bed on wheels came rolling in. "May I have some assistance?" he asked. Two men came forward; with the steward and the security guard, they lifted the man's body and got it onto the bed. They wheeled the bed up to the front. The steward spoke on the phone again; the door opened, the steward threw out the rope. Presently the wheeled bed, with the fat man on it, rolled through the doorway and disappeared.

The steward turned. "Ladies and gentlemen, I can now inform you that this boat drill has been held for a special purpose. The purpose is to isolate the carrier of the epidemic, in order to allow the other passengers to resume their normal activities. As you know, the disease is quite harmless—"

"Wait a minute," called a white-haired woman. "Are you saying that we're all quarantined on this boat?"

"That is unfortunately the case. However, this merely means that each of us, including myself, will be here until they become ill, and then we will spend ten days in the hospital receiving the best of care."

There were other voices, but she hardly heard them. It was clear now that she had made an unforgivable mistake: she had underestimated her opponents.

Was it possible that they were now prepared to let one of their number die in order to be rid of her? If so, her destiny had turned, all in that single unsuspecting moment when she had walked into the lifeboat; the game was lost, her death certain, her children unborn.

38

The steward spoke on the phone again, then turned and faced the passengers.

"Mrs. Claiborne?"

"Here," said the young woman opposite.

The steward came and bent over her. "May I see your ID, please?" He took the cards she handed him, examined them carefully. "Will you please come with me?"

"I'm sorry, what is this for?"

"You are being released, because you have already had the disease. You will be taken to quarantine in another lifeboat, and then when we are sure that the disease carrier is still here, you will be free to go."

She looked at her husband. "Malcolm, I don't want to leave you here alone."

"No, you must go," he said, pressing her hand. "There's

no point in both of us being cooped up; don't turn martyr on me again, will you?''

She smiled. ''All right, I'll try not to. See you soon.''

The steward led her to the front of the boat. The door opened and a gray-haired man walked in. At the steward's nod, Mrs. Claiborne walked out. The door closed.

''Steward, may I ask what is happening?'' an old woman demanded.

''Yes, madam. Mrs. Claiborne has been released because she has already had the disease. This gentleman is a volunteer, to replace the gentleman who became ill. Each of us who becomes ill will be replaced in this way, and so you see, we will all be able to leave the lifeboat very shortly.''

Now their strategy was clear, and she admired it for the ingenious way it circumvented their taboo against killing. It was evident, moreover, from the lengths they had gone to, that they were not willing to sacrifice one of their number. Therefore her response must be to show that their strategy could not succeed. When they realized that, they would have to release her along with the rest of the passengers. But what if they did not?

The steward was passing, and she slipped out and across and in, so smoothly that he did not notice until he heard the woman's body fall to the floor. He knelt and straightened her out, pulled down her skirt. Her pulse was steady and slow. It was interesting, the steward thought, how stupid and ugly people invariably looked when they were unconscious.

Yeager had to get out, and he thought he knew a way to do it. If he fell over, seemed to collapse, and if he didn't move, not for anything, they would take him out on a litter. Then he could "recover" when he got to the infirmary, and once he was out, there would be no reason to put him back in again. And he would find her sitting in a restaurant, or in a deck chair by the pool, and he would say, smiling, "May I join you?"

He closed his eyes, let his body go limp. He was careful to twist a little as he went down, so that he struck the floor on his shoulder and rolled over onto his back. He lay there, schooling himself to breathe slowly, and listened to the voices around him.

The steward hurried back down the aisle. His curiosity was aroused: there was something odd about the appearance of the young man on the floor—he did not look ill, or even unconscious; he looked like someone pretending to be asleep. In the act of kneeling, he slipped out once more and in again, and when he heard the body fall beside him, he was so startled that he almost opened his eyes.

After a long time he felt himself lifted and placed on a litter. He was being rolled up the aisle; then there was a wait. The door opened. "Two of them this time," said a voice a little distance away.

"Yes."

"Well, it's going faster, anyhow."

The litter moved again, swung around, halted. He heard another door opening. He concentrated on being limp, not giving in to the temptation to look through his eyelashes. Now they were going into an elevator; the door closed, the elevator was moving. Now he was being wheeled down a long hall. Another door. "Two this time!" said a female voice. "Oh, Dr. McNulty!"

Another presence was bending over him. "Get the tube into that one, will you, Terri?" said the voice. "Something funny about this one—"

And he slipped out through the fuzzy space and in again, and as he bent over the patient he could see that he had been mistaken; the young man was in a typical stupor, eyes half-closed, breathing almost imperceptibly. He must be cracking up, thought Dr. McNulty.

39

Nothing more happened on the lifeboat for the rest of the day. At the staff meeting in the morning, McNulty said, "There's no use speculating, but what bothers me is that the thing may be deliberately holding back. Staying in one host until the victim dies."

"Can it do that?" asked Higpen.

"It did once before."

"I don't see what it would gain," said Arline Truman. There were faint brown semicircles under her eyes.

"Well, if it killed another person, we'd have to take the rest of them out of there."

"But what if we didn't? Then it would be stuck on the lifeboat."

"We'd have to," said McNulty. His face was grim.

"All right, but *it* doesn't know that. Maybe it's trying to bluff us."

"As you say, Doctor, there's not much use in speculating," said Bliss. "It may be a war of nerves. When it sees that we don't flinch, it will change hosts again and then we'll go on with the volunteers as we planned."

"Yes, and then what?" Bernstein wanted to know. "Mr. Bliss, I didn't get much sleep last night. I was thinking, what if this plan works—what then?"

"It gives us a breathing space."

"That's not good enough."

"I know it isn't. Doctor, have you had any luck with the drug idea?"

"No."

"What drug idea is that?" Bernstein demanded.

"Oh, just a thought. We wondered if there might be some common drug that would keep the parasite from invading anyone."

"The sample is too small," McNulty said. "So far I haven't found anybody who was under the influence of marijuana or barbiturates, or half a dozen other things, but that doesn't prove anything."

"What about dosing the volunteers before they go in?" Truman asked.

"Worth trying, maybe. There are thousands of drugs."

Bernstein said, "I want you to look at this. What if the drugs don't work, what if nothing works? Then there's only one way we're going to kill that parasite, and that's to kill the person it's in."

McNulty was shaking his head.

"Throw him overboard," said Bernstein. "Right down to the bottom of the sea."

"We can't do that," said McNulty almost inaudibly.

202

"Maybe we can't do anything *else*," said Bernstein. "We're going to have to face this sooner or later, and it might as well be now."

"Mrs. Bernstein, let's not exaggerate. Doctor, I had another thought—what about the period when the parasite is between hosts? Something like a crab out of its shell. Do you suppose it might be vulnerable then?"

McNulty stroked his chin. "Vulnerable to what?" he said. "Electrical fields, maybe?"

"Yes, something like that. Mr. Jacobs, could you rig up some sort of gadget?"

"Sure, if I know what you want."

"Well, more or less a little of everything. Electrical fields, ultrasound, radio frequencies, anything you can think of."

"It will look like some kind of Buck Rogers gun," said Jacobs, grinning.

"All right, but if it turns the trick, we won't mind. Is there anything else? Any other suggestions? Until tomorrow, then."

The observer was delighted with this unique opportunity to observe McNulty, the man who was charged with caring for his former hosts, and he was interested by the dim, distorted image of himself as McNulty imagined him. He admired the doctor for his humility, his lack of self-deception, and his deep anguish at having caused the death of a patient; these qualities gave his personality a flavor which the observing mind found deeply satisfying.

Through McNulty, also, he had gained insight into the characters of the other rulers of Sea Venture, particularly Bliss and Bernstein. Bliss was a conscientious and unimaginative man, an administrator. Bernstein, by far the strongest personality in the ruling circle, had nearly been the death of him. He had considered taking them both if he could, but he had concluded that it would be foolish to put them out of action, since they would be replaced by others about whom he knew nothing. Furthermore, the engineer Jacobs represented a possible threat which must be investigated.

As they got up to leave, he saw his opportunity and slipped out, across to the man waiting his turn at the doorway and in again, and the startlement and confusion crashed in around him as the body fell to the floor and someone else tripped over it.

"My God, it's Dr. McNulty!" said Bliss's voice. "Mr. Skolnik too?"

"No, I'm all right," said Skolnik, getting to his feet. "But I think he's got it."

"How is that possible?" said somebody.

"Mr. Seaver, call the hospital, please, get a litter up here."

"Do you want me, Chief?" said Jacobs.

"No, that's all right." Jacobs and one or two others walked out.

"Do you realize," Arline Truman was saying, "that this means the parasite was in Dr. McNulty all the time we were talking? It knows every single thing we said."

A horrid thought came into Bliss's mind. He said loudly, "Ladies and gentlemen, will you please all move away from one another? Get out of the doorway, if you will, back into the room . . . that's right, thank you. I'd like you to keep at least five feet away from each other. When you leave, please do so one at a time, keeping your distance." He looked around. "Who's missing? Taggart, Williams and Jacobs. Mr.

Seaver, will you please try to get them on the phone and tell them the same thing? Tell them to stay at least five feet away from everyone.''

"What's this for?'' Skolnik asked.

"The parasite is probably in one of us at this moment. We have reason to think that it can't travel more than four feet or so from one person to another. If the thing went from one to another of us, it could put the whole operating staff in hospital.''

Higpen said quietly to Yetta Bernstein, "We can't go back to perm.''

"You're right.''

"What about elevators?'' Erik Seaver asked. "And restaurants? You can't even get from one place to another in Sea Venture without coming closer than five feet to somebody.''

"In that case, don't go out. We'll do our conferences by phone if necessary. Do your work the same way as much as you possibly can. Have your meals in your rooms, and be sure the stewards don't come near you.''

Higpen attracted Truman's attention. "Arline, Yetta and I think we'd better stay somewhere until this is cleared up. Can you get us a couple of rooms?''

"Yes.'' She put her hand to her forehead. "Let me think. I'm not even sure I can get back to my office. All right. I'll call them from here, get the numbers of the rooms, and I'll have somebody open them and leave the keys inside.''

"Thank you.''

"All right, then,'' said Bliss, "if there are no more questions, will you please leave one at a time? As soon as we know where we are, I'll notify all of you.''

*   *   *

Jacobs went into his office, feeling shaken up. The thing had never attacked a staff member before, and he had unconsciously assumed that it wouldn't. He sat down, put his feet up on his desk, and began to think about Bliss's idea for a Buck Rogers gun. Electrical fields, radio hash, no problem, just an unshielded motor—a drill would do, and he could use the grip and trigger for the rest of the stuff. Diagrams went through his head. Ultrasonics, maybe not—they had an ultrasound generator in the fishery, but it was too big. Ultraviolet, though . . .

And as the observer absorbed his knowledge, he saw that none of the things Jacobs was planning could harm him. He had thought as much, but it was important to be sure. When the steward came in with the lunch cart, he slipped out again and watched as Jacobs toppled silently to the floor.

40

After Jacobs, no more of the staff were attacked. Bliss kept up the five-foot rule just the same; it was a nuisance, almost unenforceable, but he could not see what else to do. Patients were still coming in to the hospital annex, five or six a day. About half of them were stewards, and the problem there was serious. Some of the remaining stewards were flatly refusing to work, and Skolnik had been forced to offer them stupendous bonuses.

The horrifying thing was that the parasite had got off the lifeboat in spite of all their precautions. If it could do that, then perhaps everything they thought they knew about it was false. Bliss realized for the first time how much they had all depended on McNulty. Now there was nobody to take the strain but Bliss himself, and he alone knew how inadequate he was.

He saw very clearly that his failure might mean the collapse of civilization. It was all very well to say that bad behavior was due to irrational instincts, but if it weren't for instincts nobody would do anything at all. Nations would break down, the family would break down— Who would get married and have children, for instance, if they were guided only by reason?

So he had to find the way to eliminate the parasite. He knew there must be a way, but although he squeezed his brain like a damp sponge, for the life of him he couldn't see what it was.

After Emily got out of the hospital, the world began to seem very strange. Things around her were less frightening and at the same time, in some indefinable way, less interesting. The lifeboats, for example, were merely lifeboats and not wells of terror. She saw now why Jim had been so impatient with her; he could not understand why she was frightened of so many things, and now she could not understand it herself. She was not frightened of Jim, either, and that was a hard thing for both of them to get used to. He looked at her in bafflement sometimes, as if she were a stranger. They were extraordinarily polite to each other. She saw that in a way he missed the old Emily, because that Emily had needed him.

No matter where they went, she never heard the sound of the grocery cart now, and she knew it was gone forever. It was as if a kind of vacuum cleaner had taken the fuzz out of her brain. And she was grateful for that, but she saw now that her fears and delusions had been all she had. Sometimes lying awake at night she tried to summon one of them up again like a familiar old ache. But they were gone, and she didn't know who she was.

CV

Phil and Rodney Thurston were twins, eighteen years old, red-haired and green-eyed. Phil was the taller one; Rodney was a little heavier and rounder-faced. They were traveling with their father; their mother was dead. The trip, their father said, was a reward for their having graduated from the Stowe School without disgrace and having successfully crammed for Harvard. Phil and Rodney would have preferred a month in Paris, or even Denver. Half the time they walked around with SeeMan headgear on, watching the frantic images on the screen and listening to the earphones. They went to plays and concerts with their father when they had to—the old man was a bear on culture—and commented politely, because if they didn't he would go into his berserk mode. To each other, in moments of privacy, they said, "*Bor*-ing."

When their father collapsed in the Sports Deck Lounge and was carried away to hospital, things began to look up. The new atmosphere of Sea Venture was exciting, and it was wonderful to be absolutely free. At first they only stayed up all night and got drunk on whisky. Later they tried other things.

A branch whipped at his eyes as he stood up, and he jerked away with a feeling of anger and resentment, as if it was somebody's fault that he hadn't seen the branch, or had misjudged the distance. It was the kind of feeling that made you go down to City Hall and complain. What was he sore about, that his eyes wouldn't focus that close? And where was that anyway, in the woods behind his parents' house, or where?—and when had it happened? It was gone, just that little bit complete in itself but with nothing before or after.

"Put it down over there," her voice said. "It" was a stoneware jug, sweating cold, and "there" was an enamel-topped table in the potting shed. That was all, a crisp little bit of memory or desire—it could have happened, they had spent a lot of time in that potting shed, but he did not recognize it, had never thought it important enough to save, and he had no idea what came on either side of it. He spoke her name, trying to bring her back, to turn around so he could see her, and at the same time he knew that was all there was: just the coolness of the white jug in his hands, and the voice, unemphatic, not laden with any message—just "Put it down over there."

He remembered how he had thought he was prepared for Nita's death, and more than prepared—impatient for it, as an end to her pain and his. When she died, he was unready for the depth of his grief. Grief wasn't even the word; he did not perceive himself as grieving, or mourning; it was more as if he were trying to come to terms with some inarguable fact that made everything else meaningless.

It was only his work that had pulled him through it, and for months, even after he thought he was over it and was fooling everybody, there would be absolutely unexpected tidal waves of sorrow.

And he had been a better physician for it, after a while, and it had even occurred to him that every doctor who had to deal with people's pain ought to have to undergo something like this himself, maybe as part of the internship. You couldn't kill off the intern's wife, and if he was as poor as most of them he didn't have one anyway, but you could give him something he greatly desired and let him get used to it and then take it away. That would do something, maybe, for the

210

habit of reducing patients to parts of the body—"this liver," or "this melanoma," the way so many doctors did.

He dimly knew that he was a patient himself right now, must be, this sense of floating around not quite bodiless but almost, and it had the comforting feel of being too sick to go to school when he was a kid, bundled up safe and warm in bed in the little room behind the kitchen, with his mother somewhere out there ready to bring him aspirins and tea. It was that kind of feeling of not having any problems or responsibilities, just having to be sick, which was easy and pleasant to do. And drift from one place to another.

Here now was one of those places in Disneyland or wherever it was, with green stick-people climbing around in their network of spikes the color of mole fur. Their faces weren't human, but that didn't bother him the way it had before, it was just interesting, and he knew it would be easier to understand them later on—"when we are all brothers and sisters."

41

Hartman was more deeply disturbed than ever by what was happening in Sea Venture. He had seen violence before, during the London riots in the eighties, and after the Lisbon earthquake; when civil order broke down, people who were normally restrained took advantage of the opportunity to loot and break things; that was understandable. But wasn't this something different?

Boys walking up to an elderly woman, taking her cane away and using it to break her bones. Assaults with broken Coke bottles, rapes, knifings. It was senseless, purposeless violence, as if, Hartman thought, there were some dark half-aware force in human minds that saw itself threatened, and was striking out like a wounded animal.

When the call for security volunteers went out, Hartman offered his services and was given a supervisory post on the night shift. A little before midnight of his third day, he was sitting at his desk in the corridor when he saw Hal Winter coming toward him.

"Well, we meet again," said Hartman. He looked at the white armband on Winter's sleeve and the nightstick in his hand.

"You, too?"

"Oh, yes. They think I'm too feeble to patrol, but they let me supervise. They've even given me a title, the same one I had before; that's very nice in a way. Well, let me tell you the drill. Your section is the port side of this deck, midships forward, from Corridor A to E. Your partner should be here in a few minutes and he'll show you the ropes. Here's my number; you call that if there's any trouble. Do that *first*. Every hour you're allowed a ten-minute rest period here— you see I've got coffee, doughnuts, all the comforts of home. They've told you, I expect, about excessive force?"

"Yes."

"Well, don't take it too seriously. If there is any trouble, talk your way out of it if you can, but if you can't, use the baton—that's what it's for. Had any training with the stick?"

"No."

"Let me show you one or two things. If it's a man with a weapon, go for the wrist, shoulder, elbow—anything to make him drop it. Or if he's too active for that, thrust straight for the gut. The baton gives you sixteen inches reach, probably more than anything he'll be carrying. If you hit him hard enough, you'll paralyze his solar plexus, and he'll be in enough pain that you shouldn't have any trouble getting him to come along peacefully. The detention rooms are right here, down the corridor. Now say it's a man attacking a woman. In that case I wouldn't advise the talk method. Tap him behind the ear, like this, or on the temple, about hard enough to crush a grapefruit. Don't be too dainty. The idea is to stun him, or knock him out, but if you happen to give him a concussion, don't worry—better him than you. Is that all clear?''

"Yes. I hope so." Winter smiled.

"You're a big, strong lad; you shouldn't have any problems. Good luck to you.''

The first time was when they were coming back from a late movie, cutting across the residential corridors to get to the elevators on the starboard side. Ahead of them was an old woman hobbling along with a cane. "Ten points," said Rodney.

They looked at each other. Phil said, "Dare you."

Rodney said nothing, but there was a glint in his eye. He started to walk faster. Phil hurried to keep up, suddenly excited, wondering if he would really do it.

They came up behind the old woman. As they were about to pass, Rodney reached out, grabbed the cane and pulled. "Oh!" said the old woman as she fell. Her eyes were like oysters; she was still holding onto the cane. Rodney yanked it away from her. His face was flushed, his lips bright. He raised the cane and brought it down across her knees. Then they ran, with her screams behind them.

They hid the cane behind a grandfather clock in the lounge. The next night they got another one, and then every night when they went prowling, they both had their canes.

For a while they specialized in old people, but that got boring, and one night they caught a young woman alone. They backed her into a doorway and Rodney held his cane across her throat while Phil pulled her panties down. Afterward they didn't look at each other or speak; but three nights later they did it again.

Although the corridors of Sea Venture were strewn with paper and trash, ceiling lights broken, some TV screens blank, a curious semblance of normal life went on; the casino was closed, but the restaurants and bars were open; the only difference, aside from the litter, was that you met fewer people, and some of them were a little strange. Barlow and Geller, picking their times and places with some care, had never had any trouble; Geller looked just sufficiently large and bad-tempered to discourage interference, and Barlow carried a dissecting knife in her purse.

They were sitting in the Quarter Deck Bar one afternoon, drinking margaritas. "There's one," said Barlow, looking across the room. "No, both of them are."

Geller followed the direction of her gaze. "Yeah."

"They're looking at us."

"Well, why not?" Geller raised his glass and smiled.

The man was saying something to the woman. After a moment they rose and came across the lounge, carrying their drinks. "May we introduce ourselves?" said the man. "My name is John Stevens. Allow me to present Julie Prescott."

"Sit down," Geller said. "Randy Geller, Yvonne Barlow." They slid over to make room.

"You are both recovered patients of the epidemic, isn't that so?" asked Stevens.

"Number one and number two. The question is, how did you know?"

"I think it's something about your faces," Julie Prescott said. "But I really don't know how I know—I just do."

"Which of you was number one?" Stevens asked politely.

"I was. Down in the marine lab. McNulty thinks it was something that came out of an australite we dredged up. He also thinks it isn't a disease, it's an intelligent parasite."

"And you don't believe this?"

"Oh, yeah, I believe it too."

"Do you work in the marine laboratory also, Ms. Barlow?"

"Yvonne. I did—we both did—but we quit."

"I see. Because it didn't make sense anymore?"

"That's right."

They looked at each other. Barlow had a curious feeling that the words themselves were unimportant.

"Do you think that is the recognition factor, then? We recognize those to whom life no longer makes sense?"

"Not life," said Barlow. "The way we used to live."

"And how will you live now?"

Geller said, "Yvonne and I are going to set up a little private lab on the Upper Peninsula in Michigan. We can do enough commercial work to get by, and still do some real science."

"That will not be marine science, will it, in Michigan?"

"No, but biology is biology. Yvonne is interested in schistosome dermatitis. Swimmer's itch. It's a parasite, maybe that's why she likes it. What about you?"

"I'm not sure yet. I think my problem is with life in general."

Julie said, "I'm going to paint, I think. For a year or two, anyhow, long enough to find out if I'm any good."

"Always assuming we get off Sea Venture," said Geller.

Stevens smiled. "Oh, we'll get off. One way or another."

42

The makeup was Rodney's idea. With pale powder on their faces, and old-man wigs stolen from the costume shop behind the theater, wearing their father's suits, they could hobble along like two old crippos, and nobody would think twice about their canes.

One night they had a bit of bad luck. They had just tripped an old woman, and Rodney had given her a whack on the head to keep her quiet, when someone appeared around the corner and came toward them. There were two of them, men with nightsticks in their hands and white brassards on their sleeves.

Phil and Rodney looked at each other. "Sweet, play it sweet," Rodney muttered.

"What happened here?" said one of the men. "Who did this?" He went down on one knee to look at the unconscious woman.

219

Damon Knight

"Officers, it was horrible," said Rodney in his old-man voice. "These two boys came up, and, and just *hit* her with a stick."

"Which way did they go?" said the other man, moving closer. He was looking at them in a way Phil did not like.

"Down the corridor," said Rodney, pointing. He bent over, clutching his chest. "Oh, I don't feel well at all. It's my heart."

"May I see some ID?" asked the second man. The first one was standing up, talking into his phone. The second one was coming too close.

"Geronimo!" yelled Rodney, and swung his stick at the man with the phone. Phil brought his cane up hard between the other one's legs. The man hit him on the cheek with his nightstick, but Phil was dodging, and he hooked the man's leg and brought him down. Then Rodney was hitting him too, and the man was sprawling beside the other with blood coming out of his mouth. Then they ran. It wasn't till later that Phil began to feel the pain of his broken cheekbone.

Early in the morning Stevens was awakened by the buzz of the phone.

"John, I'm sorry to trouble you, but Hal hasn't come back, and I can't raise him on the telephone. They don't seem to know anything about it at security. I wonder if—"

"Of course. I'll find out what I can and call you in a few minutes."

Stevens put the phone down, then thumbed it on again, punched the hospital. After a moment a tired female voice answered.

"Can you tell me if you've admitted a patient named Harold Winter in the last few hours?"

"Let me check." Stevens waited. "Yes, he was admitted at four A M."

"May I ask his condition?"

"He's stable. It's a concussion. We'll know more in five or six hours."

"Thank you."

Stevens got up and began to dress. His actions were automatic; he was in no doubt of what he was going to do. He put a sap in one pocket, the flat leather case in another.

Ever since his recovery he had been in a half-pleasurable state of suspension. He had told Newland that he didn't believe in accidents, but that was not true. Now that he no longer valued his past, he felt that his future was exquisitely, weightlessly in balance, that any puff of air might topple him one way or the other. He had been waiting with curiosity to see if fate would send him a message. Now here it was.

He knocked on Newland's door. "Paul, it's John."

"Just a moment."

Newland opened the door. He was in his wheelchair, still dressed in pajamas. "What is it, is he hurt?"

"Yes, I'm afraid so. They want me to bring you down—he's conscious, but they can't move him."

"Oh, God," said Newland. His voice broke. "How did it happen?"

"They're not sure. Somebody attacked him, down on the Boat Deck." He closed the door behind Newland and walked beside his chair to the elevator.

"The *Boat* Deck?" said Newland.

221

"Yes, they changed his section this morning." The elevator took them down; the door sighed open.

Stevens led him to the lifeboat bay. It was dark there; one of the ceiling lights had been broken.

"Here?" Newland asked, peering in, just before Stevens hit him with the sap. The old man slumped over; there was no blood.

Stevens wheeled him into the alcove. He took the flat plastic strip out of its case, slid it into the lock. The door opened; he pushed the chair through, closed the door behind him, then opened the second door, the one to the boat itself. The lights and air conditioning came on as they entered.

Stevens left the chair in the aisle and went forward to the pilot's console while he pulled on his gloves. Through the thick portholes he could see wind-driven spray dashing against the hull. In his mind's eye he saw the boat slide out of its tube, plunge into the water, bob up, then slowly drift astern. Not bad: a Viking's funeral.

Newland was breathing slowly and shallowly. He was not dead yet, but soon.

Stevens returned to the access panel beside the door, removed it, and examined the controls. He flipped the switch marked SIGNAL OFF. He set the timer for two minutes and turned the AUTO LAUNCH control to the ON position. He left the access panel on the floor. With a last glance at Newland's gray head, he went out the way he had come.

For two minutes nothing happened in the lifeboat. Then the timer clicked. The umbilicals were uncoupled and with-

222

drawn. The hydraulic ram on the far side of the boat slid back, releasing the boat; compressed air blew it out of the tube. The engine fired automatically, propelling the boat to windward, away from Sea Venture.

43

There was a blinking red light on the console. Ferguson said to Bliss, "We have a door signal from Lifeboat Fifty-three."

"Another malfunction?"

"Probably."

"Send a person down to check it out."

A few minutes later Ferguson exclaimed, "Now we've got a launch signal from the same boat!" He pressed buttons rapidly. "No status signal," he said after a moment. "I think it's really launched, although how that could happen—"

Nothing but rain and spray was visible in the windows or the television screens. "See if you can pick up anything on radar."

"Too much chop," said Ferguson. "There could be a dozen lifeboats out there and we'd never see them."

Without waiting for orders, Stuart was speaking into her

225

microphone. "Sea Venture calling Lifeboat Fifty-three, do you read? Come in, Lifeboat." After a while she turned and shook her head.

Bliss stood where he was, trying to look as if he were thinking. Good God, what was he going to do? What would Nelson have done? If the lifeboat had actually been launched, either it was a malfunction, meaning there was nobody aboard, or someone had managed to launch it deliberately. In that case there was a small but measurable possibility that the passenger was carrying the parasite.

What next? There was no drill for Sea Venture to retrieve a lifeboat; the designers had assumed that if the boats were launched, it meant that Sea Venture was foundering. The only thing he could do was to launch a second lifeboat, but that meant doubling the chance that the parasite would get away. It would be a dicey thing for anyone to get from one lifeboat into another in this weather; if the first boat turned out to be empty, he might have drowned a man for nothing.

Stuart said, "Chief, Quinn reporting from Lifeboat Bay Fifty-three. The boat's gone."

"Get me the hospital annex."

"Annex, Fenwick," said a woman's voice.

"This is Chief Bliss. Have you had a new epidemic patient in the last half hour?"

"No, sir."

"Call me the moment you do."

An hour went by before Stuart said, "Call for you, Chief. It's Fenwick at the hospital annex."

Bliss thumbed over the phone. "Yes, Ms. Fenwick?"

"Chief, you asked me to call you as soon as we had

another epidemic patient. One just came in. Her name is Gearhart.''

"No mistake about the symptoms?''

"No, sir.'' Her voice sounded offended.

"Thank you.'' Bliss turned to Stuart. "Send this on the emergency channel. 'Lifeboat accidentally launched from Sea Venture at'—give the position and time. 'May have passengers aboard.' Keep sending that until you get a reply.''

"Yes, sir.''

Newland awoke, dizzy and in pain. At first he did not know where he was or how he had got there. He was sitting in his wheelchair, wearing nothing but pajamas, and he was cold, and being rocked back and forth, and there was a throbbing pain at the side of his head: when he put his hand there, he could feel a huge, tender swelling.

Then he saw the yellow ceiling and the blue seats, and he thought, I'm in a lifeboat. But he did not know why. Hal had been hurt, that was it—the thought came back with a pain sharper than the one in his head. And he had called John Stevens. And that was all; the rest was gone. Had something happened to Sea Venture? Then why was he in a lifeboat by himself?

He drove his chair up to the console and looked out at the gray sea. The boat was rocking in the waves, throwing him from side to side with each motion. Newland managed to lever his body out of the wheelchair and into the pilot's seat; the effort left him weak and dizzy.

When he turned the wheel, the blunt nose of the lifeboat came around into the waves. Now the rocking motion was from bow to stern, and the gray water slapped up over the

227

portholes. He peered through the flying spray, hoping to catch sight of Sea Venture, but saw nothing. He continued turning the wheel until he had made a circle. The gray ocean was empty.

It occurred to him to look at the clock. It was ten after twelve. It had been about seven in the morning, he remembered, when he had called John. So he could not have been in the boat more than five hours. How far could he have drifted in that time?

He found the radio controls, switched on the receiver and tuned it up and down the band. Nothing but static. Which were the emergency channels? He could not remember. He turned on the transmitter and said, "Mayday, Mayday. This is Paul Newland in a lifeboat from Sea Venture. I don't know where I am. I left Sea Venture about seven-thirty this morning. Please help me. Mayday, Mayday."

The boat rocked and plunged as it crossed the waves. Newland strapped himself in. His legs were hurting him very much.

44

Carl Nohrenberg went through the metal detector and the explosives sniffer, showed his ID to the Marine guard, and entered the Oval Office at precisely eight-fifteen. The President, as usual, was sitting behind the Mickey Mouse figures at his desk, impeccably dressed, ruddy, cheerful, and smiling.

"Well, what have you got for me this morning, Carl?"

Nohrenberg opened his folder. "Mr. President, we have a very strong statement in support of your Zaire policy from President Lamartain."

"That's good. What else?"

Nohrenberg turned over a page. The President always liked a couple of pieces of good news to start off with. "We have an advance copy of the Walter Commission report. They're going to exonerate Rickard."

"Fine, fine. Send him a fax of congratulations—no, never

mind, I'll call him myself. And nowww,'' he drawled, with a grin, "what's the bad news?"

Nohrenberg smiled in return. "Not exactly bad news, Mr. President, but we're getting some more pressure on behalf of the people on Sea Venture."

"Firestein, Greaves, and about fifteen others?"

"Yes, sir, and our thinking is that it would be a good idea to accommodate them. I have Admiral Penrose penciled in to talk to you about it at ten-thirty. If you agree, he could have a helicopter carrier there in five to six hours."

"Okay, I'll talk to him. Say, that reminds me of the one about the captain whose ship went down in a storm, and the next morning he found himself floating on a raft with this parrot. . . .''

"What happened to you, lad?" said Hartman.

Winter tried to smile. His head was wrapped in bandages, and there was a deep discoloration under one eye. "I don't remember. I must have forgotten your advice. What about Ned Mulhauser—my partner? They won't tell me anything."

Winter hesitated. "He's a bit worse than you, but he'll be all right," he lied. In fact, Mulhauser had serious internal injuries and was not expected to live.

"That's good," said Winter. "Will you call Professor Newland and let him know where I am?"

"Yes, I'll do that. And I'll be back to see you soon."

Hartman tried to call Newland's suite; there was no answer. That seemed odd. He went up to the Signal Deck and knocked on the door, waited, then tried the knob. The door was unlocked. The room was empty.

* * *

CV

Oh-seven-hundred was when the home office generally liked to call, for its own inscrutable reasons. Colford, the General Manager, was very polite and helpful, but Bliss had a feeling that he did not understand the situation. "Mr. Bliss," he said this morning, "I think I'd better tell you that we've had representations from the White House on behalf of eighteen of your passengers. They would like to be assured that you'll find some way to contain this epidemic before you reach Guam."

"I can't promise that, Mr. Colford."

"*Or*," said Colford, "that in any event you'll allow certain passengers to debark, including those eighteen whose names I've already mentioned. Now I don't think that's an unreasonable request. Do you think it's unreasonable, Mr. Bliss?"

The trouble was that he couldn't tell Colford the whole truth, because he would not be believed. If he started to babble about intelligent parasites and so on, he was perfectly sure that Colford would give him the sack. Then Bliss would have to refuse to surrender command, and there would be the devil to pay. "No, that's not unreasonable," he said.

"Now, I'm told that the Navy is going to dispatch a helicopter carrier to rendezvous with you and take on your eighteen passengers, or thirty or forty, whatever it may be—I leave that up to you, Mr. Bliss. And they'll keep those people in quarantine until they're sure there's no problem, and then land them ashore. Your ETA at Guam is what?"

"Thirteen February," said Bliss.

"All right, then, will you make the arrangements, please? And, by the way, the helicopter will also bring you some medical people; that ought to relieve your mind."

"Yes," said Bliss.

231

*   *   *

Stevens' attitude toward Julie was undergoing a change
which puzzled and disturbed him. He was discovering an
absurd beauty in certain aspects of her face and body which
had seemed quite ordinary before. Apart from that, he found
himself thinking with fondness of her as a person; he wished
her well, and wanted to preserve her from harm.

That afternoon, in his bed, she murmured, "What do you
want?"

"This."

"Nothing more?"

"No. What do you want, Julie?"

She was silent a moment. "I think I'd like you to tell me
the truth."

"About myself?"

"Yes."

"Suppose I were to tell you that I'm a criminal?"

"It wouldn't surprise me. What kind of criminal?"

Stevens looked at her. "You really do want to know?
Well, then, I am an assassin. That is my profession. I was
paid to come on this voyage and kill someone. Does that
satisfy you?"

"I don't believe it," she said. Then, looking at his eyes,
"Yes, I do. Who were you supposed to kill?"

"That I don't have to tell you."

She nodded. "When are you going to do it?"

"It is already done."

She said, "Now I don't know what to believe. Nobody has
been killed on Sea Venture." But he saw that she knew it
was true.

"How do you feel about it?"

232

"About being an assassin? I feel that it is a foolish way to spend one's life."

"Only that?"

"What do you want me to say, that I repent my misdeeds? I don't. I think the world is much better without certain people, but that's not the point. The only thing I am sorry for is that my life has been senseless."

"Mine too," she said after a moment.

At sunset they were standing on the Signal Deck near the bow, looking out at the darkening sea and the rim of orange fire.

"Is that a ship?" she said.

He shaded his eyes with his hand. "Where? Oh, I think I see it. That little speck." His heart had jumped, just for a moment, when he thought it might be the lifeboat. "They are looking at us too, I suppose, and congratulating themselves not to be here. When they get home, they'll tell their friends, 'We passed within ten miles of Sea Venture.' " It couldn't be the lifeboat, of course; they wouldn't even be able to see it from this distance. He wondered if the old man was dead by now; he must be. Why hadn't he made sure? Probably, he thought, because he didn't want to be sure. He had wanted Newland to have a chance, even if only one in a hundred. If Newland had won, if he had been found alive, that would have been another signal, the one he was waiting for now.

They turned and began to walk around the pool. "Do you think we're going to make it?" Julie asked conversationally.

"The human race? I would say that depends on whether we deserve to survive."

"That's pretty cynical."

233

"No, it is very idealistic. There is a way in which some-one here on Sea Venture can save humanity very simply, if he chooses; the only question is, will he do it?"

"And what might that be?"

"There are occasions when someone knows he is the carrier of the parasite, because no one else is near enough to the last victim. At that moment, that one person has the option of saying, 'Please clear a path for me to the passenger entrance and open the door.' "

"I see. And step out? Very simple."

"Yes, very simple."

"Would you do it yourself?"

He shrugged. "If I answered yes, it would be braggadocio. Since I have already had the disease, I am not likely to be called upon. Nor are you. So we can theorize in perfect safety, and turn our backs on the problem like everybody else. Shall we go now and have some dinner?"

45

At twelve hundred hours the next day, when Bliss was just sitting down to a solitary lunch, his phone buzzed.

"Yes?"

It was his secretary's voice. "Mr. Bliss, we have an incoming video call from the President."

"Oh, God," said Bliss. He got up and went to the desk phone, turned it on. The image of an earnest crop-haired young man appeared on the screen.

"Ah, Captain Bliss? Will you hold, please, for the President of the United States?"

"I will, yes."

Several minutes passed; then the famous features appeared on the screen.

"Captain Bliss, as you know, I've been hearing a great many expressions of concern about your situation, and I want you to know that I'm ordering the aircraft carrier *Bluefields* to leave station and rendezvous with you sometime tomorrow. They will be searching for your missing lifeboat, and they'll be carrying a group of Navy doctors and nurses as well as a detachment of Marines to keep order in Sea Venture, and you'll get every aid and assistance we can possibly give you.''

"Yes, Mr. President.''

"And, Captain Bliss, the *Bluefields* will also have orders to take off as many passengers as they can who are not affected by the disease. We'll send you a list of those passengers later today, and this is a tentative list, and you can add to it from those passengers who want to go, up to the limit of what the *Bluefields* can carry.''

"Mr. President, may I ask what will be done with the passengers?''

"Yes, you certainly may, and I was coming to that. They will be kept in quarantine on the *Bluefields*, of course, until our medical people are sure everything is all right, and then they'll be taken to Guam.''

"Thank you, Mr. President.''

"That's all right, Captain Bliss, and if there's anything else we can do for you, I want you to call my office, night or day, at any time. Now I'm going to let you get back to your duties, Captain, and I want you to know that our prayers are going out to you.''

"More trouble on the stricken Sea Venture,'' said the anchorperson, looking gravely at the camera. "While a helicopter carrier steams to the rescue, a famous passenger, Paul Newland, mysteriously disappears. We'll have these and other stories after this message.''

CV

*   *   *

That evening over dinner with Hartman, Bliss said, "I'm at my wit's end, frankly. We've tried everything on earth, and it's all been a disaster. Now the thing's got off the lifeboat. That couldn't have happened, but it did. And the worst of it is that it's got McNulty, and Jacobs too. Jacobs was going to build us a gadget, to spray the thing with radio frequencies and so on while it's between victims."

"Do you think it took Jacobs to keep him from making the gadget?"

"Or to make us think that was the reason. Well, mustn't be depressing. Try this claret."

Hartman took a sip, tried not to let his opinion show on his face. "Very nice."

"It's all up to me, you know," Bliss said. "I wish it had been anybody else."

"It is a bit of a quandary, isn't it?" said Hartman. "You can't let anybody off Sea Venture until you've got rid of the parasite, but on the other hand you can't keep them here forever."

"My masters have instructed me to let a carrier take off certain selected passengers. I can't do it. If the thing once gets onto a ship that carries helicopters, there'll be no holding it."

"No, I see that. I suppose in the end it's going to come down to heroic measures. Nelson at Copenhagen, that sort of thing."

"There's the rub, I'm not a hero."

"No, well, none of us are until it comes to the point, are we?"

237

46

At oh-two-hundred that night his bedside phone *brrr*ed. More or less awake, Bliss picked it up. "Yes?"

"Chief, sorry to disturb you, but it's collect from your wife."

"On video?"

"No."

"All right, put her on."

"Stanley?"

"Yes, dear."

"We've been so worried about you, are you all right?"

"Yes, I'm fine."

"Well, dear, I wouldn't have called at this hour, but I couldn't get through before—they kept saying all the circuits were busy."

"Yes, they probably were. Is anything wrong?"

"Well, it's nothing really, but Tommy is in a little trouble.

239

He borrowed some money from a man at work, and then, you know, he lost the job and so of course he couldn't pay it back.''

"How much money?''

"Well, they say it's three thousand pounds, and you know with the new furnace last year, and the rise in the rates, it's left us very short indeed.''

"How much has he got left?''

"Well, only a few pounds, you see he lent most of it to another man, I'm afraid it's a complicated story. But this man, the one he borrowed from, is being very nasty, calling day and night, and we really are at our wit's end, dear. I just wanted to know if there's anything you can do.''

"I'll wire the money,'' said Bliss.

"Thank you, dear, you are an angel. What about your epidemic, is there anything new?''

"No, it's the same.''

"Well, I know you'll come through it all right, dear. Oh, by the way, old Mrs. Frye particularly wanted to be remembered to you. She prays for you every night, and of course we do too.''

"Thank you.''

"Well, dear, this is costing the earth. I'll ring off now. Sleep well.''

"Yes, you too.''

"And I'll give your love to Tommy, shall I?''

"Yes. Good night.''

At oh-eight-hundred the next morning, Bliss entered the Control Center as was his custom; Deputy Ferguson had just come on shift. Stuart was at the communications console.

"Mr. Ferguson and Ms. Stuart, I regret to tell you that I have been ordered to do something that in my judgment would be extremely dangerous."

"Yes, Chief?" said Stuart.

"A U.S. aircraft carrier is steaming towards us from Guam and will arrive at approximately oh-nine-hundred."

"Yes, sir."

"The carrier is to take off a number of our passengers and keep them in quarantine. I don't think they realize the impossibility of doing so on a carrier, but naturally I have no choice but to comply."

"No, sir," said Stuart.

"In the circumstances, it is regrettable that you should have informed me that our communications gear is down, and that we cannot send messages."

"Sir?"

Bliss put a finger beside his nose. "Something to do with the aerial, I believe. In fact, it's quite serious, because we can receive messages on the emergency channels, and weather and navigation signals, but no other incoming messages at all—no telephone, no TV. Naturally I expect you to make repairs with all deliberate speed. Do you understand me now?"

"Oh. Yes, sir, I think I do."

"Good. And you, Mr. Ferguson?"

"Yes, Chief."

A light was blinking on the comm console. Stuart flipped a switch and listened. "Chief, a message from the *Bluefields*. They say they will make rendezvous at oh-nine-thirteen. They're asking for confirmation."

241

"It's a pity we can't answer, isn't it? Prepare for submersion, Mr. Ferguson."

"Yes, sir."

Sirens went off all over the open decks. Stewards hurried about stowing away loose gear and escorting passengers inside. The weather doors were shut and dogged. The fishery and marine sections were secured. "Ready for submersion, sir," said Ferguson. Bliss did not reply.

At oh-nine-hundred Stuart said, "A radio message from the *Bluefields*, sir. 'We are approaching rendezvous. Do you read? Please open telephone link.' "

"Thank you."

He turned to Ferguson. "Can you see them?"

"Yes, sir. There they are." He pointed to the TV screen.

"Bone in their teeth," remarked Bliss.

"Yes, sir."

"They must be rather irritated."

"Yes, sir."

In the screen, the carrier was now plainly visible, a hulking gray shape. Lights were winking from her foremast structure.

"She's signaling by heliograph, Chief."

"I see she is. Can you read that, Mr. Ferguson?"

"Yes, sir. 'Prepare to receive helicopter.' "

Bliss frowned. "How long is it since you learned heliograph, Mr. Ferguson?"

"Thirteen years, Chief."

"So you're bound to be a little rusty. You're really just guessing at the message, aren't you?"

"If you say so, Chief."

"I do say so. In fact, we don't know that's a U.S. Navy

242

vessel at all. It could be hostile. I think we must consider evasive action, Mr. Ferguson.''

They watched in silence as the carrier rapidly drew nearer. It hove to half a mile away; there were further signals. Then they saw a helicopter lift off the deck and swing toward them.

"Down to plus ten," said Bliss, "smartly, Mr. Ferguson."

"Yes, sir."

The water rose until only ten feet of Sea Venture's upper works stood above the surface. The copter was still droning toward them. In the view from the camera on the foretop they saw it fly over, vastly foreshortened; it reappeared, circled twice, and turned back to the carrier.

"There'll be hell to pay for this later," Ferguson remarked.

"I know it," said Bliss. In the old days on the *Queen*, a first officer would not have spoken to his captain in quite that way, but Bliss wasn't a captain and this wasn't a ship.

47

On the bridge of *Bluefields*, Commander Leonard W. Markey watched in the television screens as the copter turned back from the submerging vessel. Beside him was the Executive Officer, Glenn Pugliese. The speaker crackled: *"Returning to ship."*

"Roger."

"What the hell do they think they're up to?" Markey said.

Pugliese, who knew his captain, did not reply.

"Send the pilot up for debriefing as soon as he gets here. No, belay that. Hell! I'm going to my cabin."

Bliss waited half an hour and then gave the order to surface. Presently the helicopter came out again. "Down to plus ten," said Bliss. The helicopter circled, dropped something, and went back to the carrier. "What is that?" said Bliss.

"Dye marker," Ferguson replied.

"Oh, I see. Well. That's a pity."

Twice more they surfaced, and the copter came over, and twice more they submerged. Bliss could imagine the messages flying back and forth between here and Washington.

The yellow stain spread out around them; gradually they left it behind. In the late afternoon the copter came over again and renewed it. After dinner, which he ate in blessed tranquillity, Bliss came back to the Control Center. Deputy Davis was on duty. The stars were bright over the ocean.

"Submerge to minus three hundred, Mr. Davis," he said.

"Three hundred, sir." The cub gave him a worshipful look.

"Keep her there until twenty hundred hours tomorrow. Log it."

"Yes, sir."

And now he was counting boxes in a storeroom, good lord, when was that? Seventy-nine or eighty, probably, his freshman year in college, a summer job, pure monotony, but the boxes were absolutely real now, he could even read the printing on the brown cardboard, "TEKTRONIX Decoupler, Model 105, 4920-29." He hadn't thought of that in years, and certainly hadn't remembered the lettering on the boxes, but he knew it was right. He could see his own hand with the pencil, and the clipboard, and he could see the dust motes swimming in the sunlight from the one high window.

Now the bright sparks were streaming past him, not dust motes anymore, and there was a wet smell in his nostrils, a clean cold underwater smell as familiar as bacon and eggs, and he felt his jaws snap as something came by. And now a fish swam up to him in the water that was colorless and pure as air; its scales were like multicolored armor, and it turned to look at him with one round idiot eye, then flicked away and swam to the other end of the tank.

Newland woke without knowing that he had been asleep. His body hurt all over. It was dark outside; he was very thirsty. He managed to get out of the pilot's seat and into his wheelchair; he drove it back down the aisle, found a water fountain, and drank. He thought that he probably ought to eat something. He could see the food-storage lockers over the microwave ovens, but they were out of his reach.

48

Commander Leonard W. Markey was a stocky blond man. His eyes were pale blue; his eyelashes were almost white, and his skin so fair that it burned and peeled. He would have been well suited to North Atlantic or Arctic duty, and therefore, as a matter of habit and tradition, the Navy had assigned him to the Asiatic Fleet.

Markey had graduated from Annapolis seventeen years before, standing one hundred forty-first in his class. At the age of thirty-nine, he knew he had been a little too long in grade, and could not look forward to further advancement unless there was a shooting war, an eventuality for which, as a sensible man, he had no yearning. He considered himself a good officer; in maneuvers last spring, *Bluefields* had scored the second-highest marks of any helicopter carrier in the fleet. On the whole, he was satisfied with his life and his career; he looked forward to another few years of undistinguished service, then retirement with his wife and children on Oahu.

His present mission had started out as something just unusual enough to be interesting, but certainly not much of a challenge. The search for the missing lifeboat was routine; the recon helicopters came back every day with nothing to report, and that was not surprising: if the lifeboat was under power, it could be anywhere in a thousand-mile radius by now. That was not really his problem—other ships and planes out of Guam were looking for the lifeboat, and eventually one of them would find it. Meanwhile, rescuing the VIP passengers from Sea Venture *was* his problem.

At first he had not been able to believe that CV's behavior was anything but some kind of dumb mistake, but now he was beginning to see the matter differently. This was not an aid-to-civilians mission, like ferrying Roosevelt's dog home from Yalta during World War II; he was fighting a naval engagement against an opponent who was making a jackass out of him.

The problem was that he couldn't land a copter on CV's deck, because every time he tried, the damn thing submerged. With helicopter reconnaissance, he could locate it every time it surfaced, but he couldn't fire a shot, couldn't drop depth charges, couldn't do anything that might injure civilians; and if the copter approached, down it went again.

There had to be a solution. There was; Markey had found it, and he felt pleased with himself.

For the time being, Bliss had decided, the best thing would be to run partly submerged at night, when the chances of being sighted were almost nil, and surface in daylight. There was no way to escape the carrier except by running fully submerged indefinitely, and he couldn't do that because the air-purifying chemicals wouldn't hold out forever. Food was going to be a problem, too; their supplies were meant to last only until they reached Manila.

When he entered the Control Center at oh-eight-hundred on Thursday, the sun was well up in a partly overcast sky. He said good morning to Ferguson and Stuart, looked at the log, then the barometer. "No sign of our friends yet?" he asked.

"Not yet. Woop, excuse me, I think I see them."

In the foretop monitor, a dark shape was rising and dipping near the horizon. "Yes, there they are," said Bliss. "Everything secured?"

"Yes, sir, as you ordered."

"Any complaints from the passengers?"

"Oh, yes."

The four frogmen were mustering on the flight deck. In the bridge monitors, Markey watched them climb into the copter carrying their gear. The door closed.

"*Charlie Hatrack Four Niner, you are cleared for take-off,*" said the speaker.

"*Roger.*"

After a moment the two sets of blades began to turn; the ungainly machine rose from the deck, hovered, swiveled in midair, and tilted off toward Sea Venture.

"Down to plus ten, Mr. Ferguson."

"Yes, sir."

The water rose over one deck after another. The copter

251

made a pass overhead, swung back; then a series of dark shapes dropped from it into the water.

"What was that?" said Bliss sharply.

"Frogmen, sir. Four of them."

"No, I meant that other thing—what was it, a raft?"

"Looked like one, sir."

"What are they up to?" Bliss muttered, and gnawed a thumbnail. "Raft—they'll tie onto us— Oh, God! Surface, Mr. Ferguson, smartly!"

"Sir? Yes, sir." Ferguson touched the controls. In the lookout screen they saw the water receding; then the Signal Deck broke the surface, and as the lenses cleared they could see white water boiling across the deck. Four struggling figures were washed over the side.

"Plus ten, Mr. Ferguson. Where's the copter?"

"There, sir." The helicopter swooped overhead, descended to port, came back again.

In the screens now they could see the raft, and four dark heads bobbing in the swell a few yards off the port quarter. The frogmen and their raft were slowly falling astern. The copter circled again. Presently it hovered and lowered a sling. They watched as one frogman after another was hoisted into the copter. They left the raft behind. The copter drifted away toward the carrier.

Ferguson was clearly puzzled. "Chief, if you don't mind my asking—"

"They were going to tie onto us with a long line. We'd tow them, wherever we went. Then the next time we surfaced, they'd be there. That would be the end."

"Yes, sir." Ferguson's eyes were bright.

Bliss turned away. He was not proud of himself, and the

admiring looks of his deputies merely made him feel like an imposter. This was not his line at all, this Hornblower kind of daredevilry. Something Hartman had said, talking of Nelson, had put it into his head—Nelson at the Battle of Copenhagen, putting the spyglass to his blind eye and remarking that he couldn't read the signals. That was all right for Nelson, but not for him. Nelson had been made a viscount afterward; he was simply going to lose his job, and perhaps his life.

When the copter returned with its crestfallen crew, Markey said to his executive officer, "Goddamn it, who is that guy, anyway?"

"Civilian, I think. Maybe he was in the merchant marine before."

"Well, where did he get that cocked hat?" Markey sat down at the chart table. "Do you realize I've got to signal CINCAF and tell them we've blown it again?"

"They can't get away with this forever."

"Well, what's going to stop them?" Markey looked gloomily at the table. "Get San Francisco on the phone. Tell them I want a complete set of plans for Sea Venture, right down to the nuts and bolts. This is going to be a dirtier job than I thought."

49

After a delay of twenty-four hours, the Sea Venture plans began scrolling out of the fax machine. They made a stack more than a foot high. Markey turned them over to his engineering officer, Ed Jensen, and said, "Find something."

After dinner Jensen came to him with a printout in his hand.

"Here's what we want. We know one of their lifeboats is gone—that means there's an empty launching tube." He pointed to the diagram. "This passage is closed by the door of the lifeboat itself when it's in the tube. Back here is a watertight door. Get in there, wedge that door open, and then they *can't* submerge. If we take them by surprise, we walk into the bridge, what they call the Control Center, and that's all she wrote."

"Pretty slick," said Markey. "Yes, that might just work."

* * *

Lieutenant Avery N. Hamling, Jr., was forty-seven years old, and still the strongest diver in his group. His father, a Navy Commander and a fine swimmer, had taught him from the age of four how to push himself to his limits, and the Special Underwater Section had given him the opportunity to do so. Hamling kept himself fit, and kept his men fit, ready at any time for the most hazardous and demanding duty in the Navy.

He found Markey, Pugliese, and Jensen in the conference room. "You sent for me, Captain?"

"That's right. Sit down, Hamling, and I'll fill you in. Show him those printouts, Ed."

Jensen passed a sheaf of papers across the table. "Here's a plan and elevation of one of Sea Venture's lifeboat tubes. As you can see, it's a cylinder fourteen and a half feet across by thirty-one and a half deep. Here's the passenger entrance, twenty feet back from the mouth of the tube. It leads to a passage eight feet long with a watertight door at the end. That's where we want you to go in."

Hamling studied the diagram. "The door can be opened manually from the tube side?"

"Yes." Jensen passed him another diagram. Hamling glanced at it, then returned his attention to the tube plan. "Where's the waterline?" he asked.

"Here, right at the bottom of the tube."

"And there are no handholds—nothing to grip?"

"Not in the tube. We think there are handrails in the passage. Unfortunately they don't show on these plans. They've got to be there, but we can't tell you how close they run to the doorway."

Hamling stared at the diagrams, trying to translate them

256

into an image. "Which way does the lifeboat door open?" he asked.

"Good question," said Markey, lifting an eyebrow. "Where are those plans, Ed?"

"Wait a minute." Jensen got the stack of printouts, shuffled through them. "Here we are." He pushed across a plan and elevation of the lifeboat. "The door opens inboard into the passage, and the hinge is on the left as you face the tube."

Hamling nodded. "All right, so if there is a handrail, it'll be on the right side. Next question: Is this tube port or starboard?"

"Starboard," said Markey. He picked a photograph out of the pile of papers and showed it to Hamling. "Copter got this with a telephoto lens—you can see the empty tube right here."

Hamling examined the photograph. "When was this taken?"

"This morning."

"Looks like the swells are coming in from her starboard quarter. Every time one of those swells hits the tube, there's going to be a hell of a surge. What are the chances the weather will be calmer in a day or two?"

"Zero," said Markey. "Typhoon Tony is due to pass over us two days from now."

They were silent a moment. "If it was up to me," Markey went on, "I'd wait for decent weather. But there are civilians on board with urgent appointments. CINCAF wants us to get them off right now, if not sooner."

"When do you want us to go?"

"Oh-four-hundred tomorrow."

Hamling was silent for a minute. "We can do it."

"Sure?" asked Markey.

"Yes."

"All right, now here's the other part of the problem. We can't get near Sea Venture in daylight, and we don't dare use a minisub—they might be listening for the motors. The best we can do is drop you before dawn, as near as we can get to the position where Sea Venture ought to be when she surfaces. That's going to be partly guesswork. How close do you want to be to make that swim underwater?"

"Anything up to five miles would be good."

"All right, that we can do. If we don't, though, your men are going to have to stay in the water, holding onto the raft, until we can pick you up after nightfall. It'll be a long day."

"I understand."

50

In the cone of yellow light from the helicopter, all they could see was the raft bobbing on the swells and the gray water around it: the rest of the world was empty black. They swam to the raft and climbed in; already the copter was rising. The light blinked out, the blackness pressed closer.

As the dawn light spread over the silvery wrinkled sky, Hamling stood up on the pitching raft, supported by Martinez and Orr, and began to scan the ocean with his binoculars. For a long time nothing happened.

"There it is." The upper works of Sea Venture were thrusting above the horizon.

"How far?"

"Wait a while—she isn't all the way up yet." Hamling watched, and finally said, "Five miles, maybe six." He lowered the binoculars and tucked them into his belt pouch.

259

"You want to swim a little, or would you rather hang around all day to be picked up?"

The men helped each other on with their liquid-air tanks, checked regulators, rubbed the compound on their faceplates. Orr and Martinez opened the valves of the flotation cells. As the raft sank, the five men slipped into the water.

After the fourth hour, Hamling surfaced long enough to catch a glimpse of Sea Venture and adjust the lubber line on his compass; then they went down again to five feet. An hour later, the hull of Sea Venture loomed ahead of them. They swam toward the stern. Hamling surfaced once more and peered at the black opening just above the waterline.

As each swell struck, the gray water foamed into the tube. He timed the surges: each one took six seconds, and the tube was barely emptied before the next one went in.

He tried to visualize what was happening inside the tube. The water hurtled in at an angle, slapped the forward side, filled the open passenger entrance, then rebounded from the back of the tube and washed out again. The direction of the surge was in their favor, but the water was going in at roller-coaster speed. Unless position and timing were exactly right, a man would come back out with broken limbs or a concussion.

Hamling uncoiled a line from his waist and handed the end of it to Martinez, signaling the others to link up. He turned on his back and swam close to the hull. Overhead he could see the pearl-gray lines of the troughs going in. He let himself become part of the rhythm. He visualized himself rising, catching the surge. He did not think of failure.

He counted seconds, then turned onto his side and propelled himself upward with three powerful strokes. He felt himself hurtling inward: in the blinding smother, he reached out, caught the smooth rail just where it ought to be, and hung on with all his strength as the backwash tried to suck him out again. Gasping and triumphant, he pulled himself into the passenger corridor and tied his line to the handrail. When the next surge went out, he tugged on the line. After a moment he felt it go slack, and pulled it in hand over hand as fast as he could. Martinez, with his face mask knocked awry, came in over the sill.

When they were all inside, Hamling waded to the water-tight door at the end of the passage. The control wheel was in the center of the door. He turned it counterclockwise. It was frozen at first, then it gave. He pushed it open. While the rest of them got out of their gear, Martinez took a rubber wedge from his kit and drove it under the door with blows of a mallet. He tested the wedge with his hand and held up thumb and forefinger in an ''OK'' sign.

51

At twelve hundred hours, when the shift changed, Bliss dropped in at the Control Center for a look around before lunch. Ferguson was just being relieved by Deputy Womack; the new comm officer was Peter Gann. At twelve-fifteen, Bliss was on the point of leaving when Womack sat up straight and said, "Chief, you're not going to believe this, but we've got *another* lifeboat-door signal. It's the same one as before—Lifeboat Fifty-three."

Bliss said nothing. Now what? Could somebody have got out through the empty tube? What would be the point of that? Or—oh, God—could somebody have got *in*? "See if you can shut the door," he said.

Womack shook his head. "It's still telling me the door is open. Maybe just a malfunction?"

"No. It isn't. Try opening the door, then closing it."

"I'm getting a status signal—door opening."

"Close it."

"Door closing." After a moment Womack turned. "Still the same signal—it isn't shut."

Bliss looked at the clock. How long had it been since the signal came on? Five seconds, ten? If they were really there, what were they doing now?

Under their wetsuits, the five men were dressed in white skivvies and shorts. They took Navy Colts from their pouches and belted them on. Martinez stood guard at the entrance to the lifeboat bay; the rest, with Hamling in the lead, set off up the corridor at a trot.

"Down to plus one seventeen, Mr. Womack."

"Plus one seventeen? Yes, sir." After a moment he said, "Chief? If that door's really open, we'll flood the Boat Deck."

"I know," said Bliss.

When the next surge came, an inch of water flooded into the lifeboat bay where Martinez was standing. Instead of washing out again, the water rose. Suddenly there was a clangor of alarm bells. Martinez saw the watertight door descending just in time to grab an air bottle and shove it underneath.

In the corridor, the fluorescents abruptly went out, replaced by the sullen yellow glow of emergency lights. Life rafts dropped from the ceiling and swung at the ends of their cords.

Ahead of the four frogmen, a watertight door was descending. Hamling broke into a splashing run toward it, but he was too late. The flood reached the closed door and kept on rising.

"Let me sit here, if you don't mind, Mr. Womack," said Bliss. "You and Mr. Gann watch the foretop screens, please." Bliss sat down at the console and called up a Boat Deck status display. Watertight doors were down at both ends of Corridor Y where it intersected with cross corridors, but the door at the entrance of the lifeboat bay was not closed. A real malfunction, this time, or had they jammed it with something? The water level in the corridor was just over two feet.

"Copter in sight, Chief," said Womack suddenly.

Bliss felt a sudden paradoxical relief. That meant, at least, that he had not made a grotesque misjudgment.

Submerged, Sea Venture was like a whale, a shape as portly and to all appearance ungraceful as Bliss himself. Only Bliss, perhaps, fully realized how delicately trimmed she was, how easy it would be to make her dance.

He did a mental sum. The isolated section of the corridor was eighty feet long and ten feet wide, ergo eight hundred square feet, times two made sixteen hundred cubic. That was about a hundred thousand pounds of water—fifty tons. Was that enough? Probably, but he wanted to take no chances. Bliss reached out and turned the depth control to plus one twenty-six. Sea Venture descended gently another foot. Now the sensors showed three feet of water in the corridor.

He glanced up at the monitors. The little speck of the helicopter was plainly visible.

Bliss overrode the interlock and began to pump water out of the port-side trim tanks. He watched the clinometer, feeling the vessel tilt almost imperceptibly under him. One degree; two. It couldn't be much more, or he'd be having a lot of old people falling over and breaking their hips. He adjusted the depth control again to positive one hundred twenty-nine. Sea Venture began to rise.

Womack said, "Chief, the helicopter—!"

Bliss glanced at the monitor. It was close, but there was still time. "We must rise before we can descend," he said. In the Boat Deck screens, he could see a torrent of water pouring into the ocean. The green light on the panel that indicated the lifeboat-bay door turned abruptly red. The obstruction must have been swept away. Instantly Bliss typed in another override and raised all the watertight doors. The torrent continued. In the screens, Bliss saw five men struggling in the water. When the rush of water stopped, he lowered the doors again and turned the depth control to plus ten.

Sea Venture gently slipped under the surface, all but its upper works, as the helicopter soared closer. A few minutes later, Bliss had the satisfaction of seeing the copter lower a sling to pick up the frogmen.

52

Early in the morning the hospital annex called and told Bliss that Dr. McNulty had awakened. Bliss went down an hour later and found him looking weak and bewildered. "How do you feel, Doctor?"

"Got a sore nose," said McNulty. "Now I know what it feels like. I was dreaming. I dreamed—" He closed his eyes.

Later in the day Bliss dropped in again; McNulty was looking more alert.

"Doctor, we've missed you badly. While you were ill, we've been playing cat and mouse with a helicopter carrier— they want to take off our Very Important Passengers."

"They can't do that."

"I know, and I've been able to stave them off so far, but it can't go on forever. Our only chance is to get rid of the parasite somehow in the next few days. If anything at all occurs to you—"

McNulty shook his head. His eyes filled with tears; Bliss, embarrassed, went away.

Paul Newland realized that his deliverance was not far off. He was very weak now, and he slid down into a fuzzy half-consciousness every now and then, but in the intervals his mind seemed clear enough. He had written a note to Hal, and another one to Olivia Jessup. He had gone over his life in memory, as drowning people were supposed to do, and had made his peace with it. There were things he had done that he might do otherwise now if he had the opportunity, but they had been the best things he knew how to do at the time.

It really was quite easy to die; he would have preferred not to do it all by himself, perhaps, but that was a minor complaint. He did not expect anything afterward: he believed that his personality was a unique set of wave forms which after the dissolution of his brain would fade into the background noise of the universe. He was grateful to have had the use of this body and this mind for sixty-four years; he had realized long ago that he did not want it forever.

He was quite sure now that John Stevens must have put him into the lifeboat, perhaps on orders from Bronson's group. He felt no vindictiveness, only a kind of melancholy regret. The world was going to turn without him. Probably Sea Venture would not survive; perhaps the L-5 program would. Was that a good thing or not? He no longer knew.

He awoke from one of his periods of half-consciousness and knew that the time had come. I'm not sorry for anything, he thought, and drifted away into the long dark.

*   *   *

By midafternoon heavy swells were overtaking Sea Venture from the east; the barometer was falling. At seventeen hundred hours, Bliss ordered the upper decks cleared and Sea Venture submerged to fifty feet.

Hartman was standing with Bliss and Deputy Davis in the Control Center after dinner. He could feel a faint but perceptible rise and fall of the deck under his feet.

"Why this particular depth, if you don't mind me asking?"

"Navigational problems," Bliss said. "We could easily get a smoother ride by going a bit deeper, but the deeper we go, the more northing, and we're already far north of where we ought to be. Excuse us a moment, Davis."

"Yes, sir." The deputy stepped aside.

"Here we are," said Bliss, pointing to the red dot in the center of the display. He pushed a button. "Here's our projected course for the next twenty-four hours. As you see, we're going to pass between Rota and Tinian, and that's bad enough, but farther north the currents are a nightmare, and there's a risk of being carried into a sort of mini-gyre south of Kyushu."

"That's the drawback of steering by currents, then, isn't it?"

"Quite right, and it would be much safer to cruise these waters in the summer, but then we wouldn't get the tourist trade, so there you are."

"Well, the carrier will never find us in this weather, at least. That's something."

"Yes," said Bliss gloomily.

He played a game with Hartman and went to bed, but did not sleep; he lay and watched the illuminated inertial guidance

269

repeater opposite his bed. After an hour and a half the motion of the vessel was much worse. He picked up the phone.

"Control Center."

"Womack, take her down to seventy feet."

"Yes, sir."

Presently the motion moderated again. For there to be any at all at this depth, the waves at the surface must be a hundred feet tall. Bliss wondered where the carrier was and if it had managed to get out of the storm path.

Down here, they were blind and deaf; the inertial guidance was all they had. Up there, it was a nightmare of wind and wave.

Bliss was aware that he had done all that a man could, and more than he had expected of himself. And it was all for nothing, because he couldn't isolate the parasite and he couldn't kill it. For a long time he had clung to the unreasonable hope that Dr. McNulty would think of something when he recovered. Now he could not deceive himself any longer. In another twenty hours his supply of chemicals would run out and he would be unable to submerge; then the helicopter would land and take the passengers off: mate in one.

At oh-five-hundred he got up, shaved and dressed, and went to the Control Center. He spoke to the security guards at the door, crossed the anteroom and went in.

"That's all right, Davis, you're relieved. Go and get some sleep, or whatever you like."

"Sir?"

"I said you're relieved. Go home; that's an order."

The young man stood up slowly and left the room. Bliss went and tapped the communications man on the shoulder; he looked up, raising the earphones. "You're relieved," Bliss said. "Go on, get out."

When they were both gone, Bliss locked the door and sat down for the last time in the command chair.

Never in his professional career had he had to make a decision like this. It was not his style at all; he was an administrator, not one of your Yankee skippers quelling mutinies with a marlinspike or bringing his ship through a gale around Cape Horn. But he was squarely against it now: there were no longer two choices, only one.

He looked at the inertial guidance display on the console. Their position was a little more than three miles due east of Rota. He waited and watched the chronometer, then pressed the buttons to bring Sea Venture to the surface.

Great tub that she was, she would break up like a house of cards if he ran her ashore in this weather. He had a glimpse of bulkheads collapsing, water rushing down the corridors like a gray fist.

As he waited, he felt a vague dissatisfaction, a feeling of something unfinished. It was too bad about the radio; he would have liked to try to get a call through to his wife, just to say good-bye.

53

As the great vessel rose, waves fell over her like mountains. She dipped and shuddered, and her massive fabric groaned. Cups fell off tables, then vases from stands. Throughout Sea Venture, people sat up in bed, gasped questions at each other. The motion of the vessel around them was like a betrayal, like an earthquake. The sounds were like nothing they had ever heard. Then the loudspeakers in the corridors came to life.

"Ladies and gentlemen, this is Chief Bliss. We are experiencing some turbulence as a result of surfacing to avoid a submerged obstacle. We will be descending to a safe depth shortly. There is no cause for alarm, and the lifeboats will not be used. I repeat, the lifeboats will not be used. Thank you and good night."

*   *   *

Malcolm got up and began to dress.

"What are you doing?" she asked.

"If I have to drown, I don't want to do it in bed."

After a moment she laughed. "Come here a minute first," she said. "You know, I never realized before how much I love you."

Emily and Jim sat looking at each other. Jim's face was pale; there were beads of sweat on his forehead. "Em," he said, "I'm sorry, you know—for everything."

"You don't have to be sorry," she said. "Maybe—"

"What?"

"Maybe this is a good time to forgive each other."

McNulty woke up with a feeling of panic. At first he did not know where he was. The room was dark except for a night-light; the bed was lurching under him, and a deep tortured sound came from the walls.

He got up, stumbled to the light switch, and found his pants in the closet. In the corridor he met Hal Winter, his head still bandaged. "Dr. McNulty, what's happening?"

"Don't know," said McNulty. "Get me a chair, will you—I'm not sure I can walk."

Winter brought a powered wheelchair and helped him into it. "Where are you going?"

"Control."

"I'm coming with you."

In the anteroom they found two deputies, Ferguson and Davis, Walter Taggart, the head of engineering, several security guards, and a swarm of other people. Ben Higpen,

274

Yetta Bernstein, and Captain Hartman entered a few moments later.

Ferguson was talking on a telephone. After a moment he put it down and turned to McNulty. "He won't listen," he said.

"Who?"

"The Chief. He's in there with the door locked."

"Let me talk to him."

Ferguson got up and moved his chair to make room. "Just press the button—I've got the speaker on."

McNulty rolled his wheelchair up. "Chief, this is McNulty. Mind telling me what you're up to?"

"I'm sorry about this, Doctor," said a voice, "but there's no other way to do it. If we keep on, they'll float us, or disable us, and take the passengers off. We haven't a prayer of getting rid of that thing: you know it and I know it. The only way is to take it to the bottom with us. I'm really sorry. Please tell the others not to try to break in; I'm armed, and I'll shoot if they do."

At Ferguson's gesture, McNulty turned off the phone. The deputy said, "Mr. Taggart, can you get down into the controls and cut them?"

"Not in time to do any good. I'd say force the door and take our chances. He may be bluffing about the gun."

"What if he isn't? Suppose he fires a couple of shots into the control panel?" Ferguson turned on the phone again. "Chief, we'd appreciate a chance to talk about this. Will you open the door, please?"

"Not likely. You know I'm right, all of you."

McNulty put his head in his hands. "He is right," he

muttered. Watery images were going through his head: the cold, and the fish lips nuzzling against his dead face. . . .

Suddenly he sat up. "Oh, God," he said. "The fish!"

"Take it easy, Doctor," said Ferguson, and put a hand on his shoulder.

"No, no, you don't understand— Let me talk to him." He grabbed the phone and said, "Mr. Bliss, there's something you don't know."

"There's a great deal I don't know, but I expect I'll find out shortly."

McNulty kept talking. "You remember, after Randy Geller collapsed, there was a three-hour period before the next person felt faint?"

There was a pause. "No, I don't recall. What about it?"

"He was found beside an aquarium in the marine lab. The fish, don't you understand—the fish!"

There was a silence. "Are you suggesting—?"

"That's where it spent those three hours, it's got to be. It doesn't have to live in human beings. If you sink us, you won't be killing the thing, you'll be letting it loose."

After a long pause Bliss's voice said, "Descending to one hundred feet."

Slowly the motion of the vessel steadied; the groaning died away. The door opened and Bliss emerged. His face was pale, his eyes red-rimmed. "Mr. Ferguson, take over," he said.

"Yes, sir." Ferguson passed him with a sympathetic look, as if he wanted to say more but could not find the words. The comm person followed him in.

Bliss sat down heavily and put his hands between his

knees. "I'm sorry," he said. "I've made a mess of it. I knew I would." He looked at McNulty. "We're done for, aren't we? There's no way to get rid of the thing."

McNulty felt that it was an intolerable effort to speak. "This man needs to lie down awhile, and so do I," he said. He turned to the nearest face. "Will you call the annex and get somebody to give him a Dalmane?"

After that someone trundled him into the elevator and back down to the hospital bed, and in no time at all he was awake again. Janice was saying, "Doctor, how about a little breakfast?" The idea disgusted him, but he drank the orange juice, managed to get down a few spoonsful of oatmeal. Janice started to help him to the bathroom, but "I can walk," he said gruffly, and he could.

"Any more patients?" he asked when he got back.

"Two last night, a broken leg and a heart attack."

"Where are they?"

"Down the hall, but you're not going there. The heart patient is recovering, I set the leg and it's okay. You're a patient, Doctor, and everything is under control."

McNulty wished it were true. "How is Bliss?" he asked.

"All right. He called this morning to see how *you* were." She went away. A few minutes later she was back, followed by Higpen and Bernstein. "Ten minutes," she said firmly, and disappeared again.

Higpen looked as if he had not slept, and so did Bernstein. "Doctor," she said, "we want to talk to you about an idea, if you're feeling strong enough."

"Sure," said McNulty.

"Maybe you remember I said this before. There is a way to get rid of this thing, if one of us is willing to die."

277

Damon Knight

McNulty started to shake his head.

"I'm not talking about murder, I'm talking about somebody to be a sacrifice, a scapegoat. Suppose we get a few people to agree. There wouldn't have to be many. We'd go wherever the last victim collapsed and stay there until the parasite takes one of us."

"And then what?" McNulty asked.

"Get a crate ready. A metal crate, ten feet on a side. The person, whoever it is, gets into the crate and you give them an injection."

"I won't—" McNulty started to say.

"Wait a minute, let me finish. We put some kind of a framework inside the crate to hold the person in the middle. And then we lower the crate to the bottom of the ocean. The person dies painlessly; the parasite can't get out, and the fish can't get in. Now tell me what's wrong with it."

"It won't *work*," said McNulty wearily. "If these folks know what they're going to do, the parasite will know too, and it'll get away like it did before."

"Could you hypnotize them, so they wouldn't know?"

"Are you kidding?"

Bernstein took a deep breath. Her eyes filled suddenly, and tears began to trickle down her cheeks. "Well, if we have to kill somebody who *isn't* a volunteer—" she said in a tight, high voice.

"Scapegoat," said Higpen suddenly. "Yetta, remember the goat in the King Neptune ceremony?"

"Sure I do. What about it?"

"Dressed in a suit, riding in a cart? What if we could get the thing to go into a *goat*?"

They looked at each other, then at McNulty. "Might

278

work," he said, and felt a trickle of excitement. "The thing has never seen a goat, is that right?"

"Yes, because we kept it out of perm. Do you think, if we dressed it up in a suit again—?"

"My gosh, I just remembered something." McNulty sat up straight. "When this thing first started, we were getting a run of patients that looked unusual some way—dress, or skin color. That might have been just because the thing noticed the difference, and was *curious*."

After a moment Bernstein said, "Come on." Her jaw was set. Higpen followed her out the door.

They went to look at the goats, then talked to Miriam Schofelt, who had been the chairperson of the King Neptune Committee this year. She still had the suit they had used, a paper one made by Mrs. Omura, jacket, collar and tie all in one piece. They called Dan Taggart in engineering and explained what they wanted.

"I don't know about a metal crate," Taggart said. "Even aluminum, that'll corrode away after a while. I'd say the best thing would be to use a wooden crate and fill it with concrete, if we had any."

"I've got about a hundred bags of mix in the store," Higpen said. "Is that enough?"

"Guess so. What mix?"

"Some of it's one-two-four, some one-one-two."

"Sounds good to me. How big a crate, did you say?"

279

54

Down at the end of the lobby, people were gathering around someone who had just come in. Curious, she went that way. The watcher inside her was intrigued to notice that the center of the crowd was a black-and-white goat, dressed in a gray suit and tie, sitting in a cart. It was clear from her host's reactions that this was an amusing sight, but she was not quite sure why. The relationship between human beings and the other species on their planet was something she had never clearly understood. The goat was considered an inferior animal, but if this one was dressed like a human, did that imply that some goats had a higher status?

As soon as she was near enough, she slipped out, across the fuzzy void and in again, feeling the alien body slump as she entered. She had just time to realize that the goat was indeed a lower animal, without speech or reasoning, before the needle entered her neck.

* * *

They carried the limp body into the fishery section, where the crate was ready. The crate was partly filled with concrete; they lowered the goat into it and then poured more concrete and bolted on the top. The hoist took it out over the surging green water, lowered and released it. The crate sank and was gone, on its way to the bottom. The horror went with it.

Both windstacks had been carried away in the storm, and there was other damage above decks; the radar dishes and antennas were gone, screens and railings broken. Sea Venture could not signal, but she floated, and at last the helicopter touched down on the landing area. Bliss was there to meet the Marines when they emerged with drawn pistols.

"That won't be necessary, gentlemen," he said. "Our resistance is over; you're free to come aboard."

"Who are you?" the Marine officer demanded.

"I'm Stanley Bliss, Chief of Operations."

"My orders are to place you under arrest until the vessel is secured, Mr. Bliss. Will you go ahead of us, please?"

"Certainly."

McNulty had been watching himself with clinical attention, waiting for alterations in his outlook, and he thought he had found some. It was a little as if all the things that were important to him were weighted parts in a Rube Goldberg machine, and the weights had shifted silently and smoothly to new positions. They were all still there, but their relationships were different. His view of the universe seemed perfectly coherent, and he was comfortable with it; in fact, it seemed to him that he was viewing things more sensibly and rationally than he had before. It was funny to be seeing the situation from the inside, and even funnier that it didn't seem to make any difference that he had been expecting it.

To begin with, he was not sorry that he was a doctor, and he meant to continue in the practice of his profession if he could get away with it, but he didn't feel the same way about the rules and conventions. He had a feeling that he had been doing a lot of things just to touch base or protect himself against malpractice suits, not especially for the benefit of the patient, and not doing some other things that might have been helpful. He was discovering in himself a sudden curiosity about herbal cures, for example, and psychosomatic stuff that he had dismissed as pseudoscience. Maybe it was pseudoscience, but did that matter, if it worked?

After consultation with the carrier, it was decided that two hundred passengers would be taken off now, the rest later when *Bluefields* was joined by two more carriers. Sea Venture, now far off her course, would be assisted by tugs to reach Manila. After that Bliss was not sure what would happen. Probably they would try to fit new windstacks there in order to get the vessel back to her home port in San Francisco. It was doubtful that Sea Venture would ever cruise again; the best thing might be to break her up for scrap.

As for himself, he was more or less scrap too. He might have to face criminal charges in the States, and there would certainly be civil suits as well. If he got through all that, it was still doubtful that Cunard would take him back. He could perhaps get a job managing a hotel inland somewhere. That would suit him very well.

*　　*　　*

On their last night together, Bliss, Bernstein, Higpen, Hartman, Winter, and McNulty had a late dinner. "I must say I'm proud of the lot of you," said Hartman. "If there's any justice, you'll all go down in the history books. Even if not, you'll have the satisfaction of knowing you've met and defeated the greatest threat humanity has faced in a hundred thousand years." He raised his glass. "Here's to you. May you live and prosper."

"Now I suppose we'll never know what might have happened, if it had gone the other way," said Winter. "It's a shame we didn't find out more when we had the opportunity."

"Such as?"

"Oh, well, for instance—how does the thing reproduce?"

McNulty looked startled. "Good question. Maybe it's just as well none of the passengers were pregnant."

About twelve hundred of the passengers were taken off by helicopter, over a three-day period, and transported after further delays to Guam; the rest elected to stay with Sea Venture to Manila. The vessel seemed emptier and older than she was; there was a curious sense of decayed majesty in her lobbies and corridors, as if she were an ancient hotel about to be torn down. Some of the passengers became quite sentimental in their loyalty, and spoke with scorn of those who had "left the sinking ship."

Tugs warped the battered hull into Manila Harbor on a May afternoon. The sky was cloudless, the air hot and moist. Jim and Emily Woodruff went down the ramp together, her hand tucked into his arm. "It'll be good to get home," Jim said.

"Yes." Her expression was calm as she looked out over

the sprawling city. Jim was getting used to that. "Feeling okay?" he asked.

"Yes, Jim." And she pressed his arm, gently, as if to reassure him.

Captain Hartman boarded the ramp with a twinge of regret. It was not an experience he wanted to repeat, but, after all, it was something to tell the grandchildren about: a real sea adventure. He and Bliss had exchanged promises to meet. Perhaps they would, someday, and reminisce over their pints like two old seafaring men.

Julie Prescott boarded the ramp with her parents. Stevens was a little ahead of them; they had said their good-byes. Stevens was going to fly to Switzerland; they had arranged to meet in New York in October. "When I come back, you must not mind if I have another name," he said.

Feeling a little dizzy, she thought of something she had not told Stevens about: the circled date on her calendar, two weeks ago. She had never been this late before. She was still not sure how she felt about that, or about Stevens. Was there anything ahead for them?

Well, she thought, they would all have to wait and see.